Jock Seeks Geek

HOLIDATES SERIES
BOOK TWENTY-SIX

JILL BRASHEAR

For those who told me to stop writing silly little romance novels...
here you go!

Prologue

The theater goes dark as I climb the stairs back to my seat. Gina wanted popcorn at the last second, and because I am the best best friend ever, I volunteered to get it before the movie started. I balance the tub of popcorn in one hand as I inch along the aisle, trying not to trip over anyone's feet.

Dressed in my Batgirl costume complete with a mask over the upper half of my face in honor of the latest spinoff movie, I feel like I'm with my people in the theater. Everyone is wearing wacky costumes, some with headpieces and footwear that makes it difficult to get by them in the tight rows.

"Excuse me," I say more than once as I make my way to the center of the aisle.

Gina reaches forward and rescues the popcorn from my hands before it can become a butter-soaked tragedy on the cement floor. "Thanks," she says, all smiles as she stuffs a handful in her mouth.

I settle in my seat as the first trailer airs. "You're welcome."

"Shh," says the woman beside Gina, glaring at both of us.

"Chill out," Gina says. "It's only a preview."

The woman's face flushes in the darkness, and she leans back in her seat. I wish I had half of Gina's badassary. I'm far too polite and pleasant. Gina credits her hot-blooded Italian mother for her feistiness. I guess I have my mid-western church-going parents to blame for my meekness.

There's a tap on my shoulder from behind, and I turn around and see a teenage boy sporting face paint to look like The Joker.

"Can you move your big-ass head?" he asks. "I can't see a thing."

My jaw drops. The kid can't be any older than twelve. Shock renders me speechless, and I automatically sink in my seat, attempting to shrink myself.

I've always been too big. Too tall. Too goofy. Too quirky.

In high school, I was taller than ninety-five percent of the school, including the teachers. And it hasn't gotten any better since.

Gina smacks me on the arm. "Don't worry about him," she says. "He's a little punk." She turns around, giving him the middle finger salute.

If only I could be more like Gina, but I suffer from the affliction of people pleasing. I crave acceptance like a drug.

Subsequently, I spend the entire movie hunkered down in my seat, trying to appease a pimply-faced Joker.

When the movie is over, we all file into the lobby, gushing about the incredible performances we've just witnessed. In another life, I am a famous actor who performs all her own stunts and inspires laughter and tears on a global scale.

In this one, I am a data analyst with a comic book obsession who volunteers at our local small-town theater. Backstage.

My phone buzzes with a text and I pull it out to see a notification from my friend Harry from the office.

Harry: We are partners! Yay!

Me: Partners?

Harry: Check your email

I pull up my email app and see a new message from work. The January newsletter has gone out. It includes the monthly team building event which all employees are required to attend.

January 26 is National Have Fun At Work Day, and our company has decided to make it a mud run competition. Employees who did not list a partner for the annual events were paired with other single employees.

Sure enough, Harry and I are partners in the mud run.

My heart sinks. I've been fending off hints from Harry that he wants to be more than friends for months. Although he's sweet, I'm just not interested. And I certainly don't want to be his partner for a day of athletic competition. Between the two of us gangly nerds, we are bound to place dead last.

"What's the problem?" Gina asks, steering me out of the crowded lobby.

"Unless I come up with a date for Have Fun At Work Day, I'm partnered with Harry for a mud run."

"Not Hairless," Gina says.

I laugh despite my frustration. Gina nicknamed Harry "Hairless" because he doesn't have a stitch of hair on his bald head.

"What am I going to do?" I moan.

Gina whips out her phone. "Leave it to me." She snaps a photo of me and starts typing with flying thumbs.

Dread sinks like a stone in my belly. "What are you doing?"

"There's this great new app for finding a date for an event. It's called Holidates."

"Ugh. Sounds cheesy."

"Don't judge, Batgirl."

"I don't like dating apps." My luck has never been good with meeting men online. They are never what they say they will be. Since I'm six feet tall and a lot of men exaggerate their height, they are often disappointed when confronted with the reality of my Amazonian height.

"This one is different," Gina says. "It's only for special events, nothing long term." Gina glances up at me. "Eye color?"

I shut my eyes stubbornly. "You don't know my eye color? We've been friends for years."

"So, sue me," she says. "Blue?"

I open my eyes and widen them at her. "Brown."

"What qualities do you want?" She squints up at me. "Tall, obviously. What else?"

"Funny." That one is easy. I'd rather have a man make me laugh than turn heads with his good looks. "Athletic."

Gina raises a brow. "Since when?"

"Since this is a mud run competition, and I want to win." I peer over her shoulder. "You're putting a picture of me in my Batgirl costume?"

"Why not? You look hot."

"I'm wearing a mask."

"Ups the hotness factor. Trust me." She swipes her finger over the screen. "Tall. Funny. Athletic. Done."

"What have I gotten myself into?"

Gina takes my arm and leads me out of the movie theater. "Better text Hairless and let him know Batgirl has a date."

CHAPTER 1

Thirst Trap

"**I**f it weren't for this," Becca says, pointing at her protruding belling. "I'd be your date." She places her hand on top of her rounded belly in the quintessential mom-to-be pose. "I don't think anyone would believe I'm your girlfriend."

I'm so desperate, I'm willing to coerce Becca into coming with me. But traveling to Vegas in her late stage of pregnancy definitely isn't a good idea. "I don't have time to find anyone," I say. "Maybe I'll just go alone."

Becca frowns. "You'll never be able to do this on your own."

Frustration balls in the pit of my stomach. "Thanks for your vote of confidence."

She cocks her head at me. "You know nothing about comic books."

It's true. I've never found them interesting. I'm more of an action movie guy than a reader. Evelyn would have been perfect for this. She is up on everything pop culture. But Evelyn is gone. I'm on my own, and horribly unequipped to

5

impress a client at the biggest comic book convention on the continent.

"You need a geeky wing-woman who can impress Mr. Kline."

She's not saying anything I don't know, so why does it sting so much to know I can't do this on my own?

I push away from my desk and stand. "I'm getting some coffee," I tell Becca. "You should go home."

"Have you eaten anything since breakfast?"

I have to pause and think. I can't remember the last thing I ate. Did I eat breakfast? I can't say. I've been so slammed; I've hardly stopped all day.

Becca pulls out her phone. "I'll order you something. You need food before more coffee."

I smile down at my assistant. "You're gonna make a great mom."

She swipes her finger over her phone without looking up. "I had plenty of practice being the oldest of six." Glancing up at me, she frowns. "I hate to leave you here by yourself."

"No worries." I'm used to being here by myself. Ever since Evelyn left and took over half our employees with her, I'm used to being on my own during odd hours, trying to glue together all the loose pieces.

"Pizza okay?" Becca asks.

"Sure." I don't care what I eat. Everything tastes like cardboard these days. I make my way into the break room and push the button on our fancy coffee machine. It's one of the few things Evelyn left behind. She even kept the expensive engagement ring I gave her. Thank God I didn't give her my grandmother's ring. I'd somehow known she wasn't the right woman to wear it.

"I have a brilliant idea," Becca says, leaning in the doorway.

"Pepperoni is fine."

"I'm not talking about your food order." She shows me her phone. "Check this out."

I glance up from the coffee maker and peer at her phone. The meager scraps of my good mood evaporate.

"I don't do dating apps." My voice comes out a little harsher than I'd intended, and I soften it immediately. No need to make a pregnant woman cry. I can't stand for any woman to cry, much less one who is growing a human inside her. "Thanks for trying."

"This isn't an ordinary dating app." Becca shoves the phone in my face. "It's specific to people who need dates for events."

I cringe so hard I feel my skin crawling. "Losers who can't get a date on their own."

"Well..." Becca reaches over to pat my forearm. "You're going through a rough time. It happens."

It's never happened to me before. I've never had a hard time getting a date. But since Evelyn, I'm off my game. And the game isn't something I'm eager to return to.

"I don't need a date," I say. I can research everything I need to know about comic book superheroes in the next few days and show up at the Las Vegas convention ready to play. Ready to win Kline's business.

At heart, I'm a competitive athlete. I can figure out any game.

"I'm sorry, Vince, but you do." Becca takes her phone back and swipes her fingers over the screen with record-breaking speed. "How about this?"

She shows me her phone again, and I nearly spit out the sip of coffee I just swallowed. "Where did you get that picture?"

I'm looking at a photo of me. Shirtless.

"From the retreat last winter," Becca says. "We were all at the pool."

"No one gave you permission to take that."

"You're a total thirst trap," Becca says, pulling the phone from my grasp. "Let me just cut off your head."

"What's wrong with my head?"

"Nothing's wrong with your head, but it creates intrigue if they can't see your face." She eyes me in a way that makes me think something is on my face, then returns to tapping and swiping. "Trust me."

"You're not starting a profile for me."

"Already done," she says, grinning.

Despite my protests, the idea of a mutual exchange of favors is intriguing. It's not a date so much as a trade. There are no expectations, no pretenses, no lies. Unlike my previous relationship.

"I'm writing the description now," Becca says. "How would you describe yourself in three words?"

Heat rises up my neck. I have no idea how to describe myself, much less in three words. Before Evelyn, I would have been able to come up with an entire list. But she broke my heart and stole my shine as well as half my clients.

When I don't answer right away, Becca taps into her assistant superpowers. "How about confident, athletic, and stylish?"

My chest puffs up at this description. I'm glad she noticed my style. These Italian suits aren't cheap. Given my height and girth, I have to get them custom made.

"Oh! Look!" Becca bounces on her toes. "You've got a response already."

"What?" I peer over her shoulder at her screen. "How?"

"It's the six pack."

"Great."

My sarcasm goes unnoticed as Becca focuses on her phone. "No. She won't do."

I feign nonchalance, but I'm dying to know all the details.

From over Becca's shoulder, the woman's photo looks pretty good to me. She's curvy and brunette, nothing like Evelyn. Perfect.

"What's wrong with her?"

Becca squints at the photo. "She's obviously a catfish." She swipes the screen and shakes her head, dismissing women who don't make the cut.

As long as we are doing this, we need to do it right. "She needs to know comic books," I say.

"On it."

"And she needs to be decent looking."

"Of course." Becca cuts her eyes at me. "No one would believe you'd go for anyone less than a six."

I lift a brow. "That's rude"

Becca nods and bends her neck over her phone. "But true."

She scrolls for a moment, and I feel ridiculous. Nervous for no reason. This isn't about finding a relationship. It's about finding a way to better my chances with a client by fitting in at a comic book convention.

"How about her?" Becca shows me the screen.

"She's wearing a mask." I turn away from the phone and stride down the hall toward my office. "I don't think this is a good idea."

Becca follows me, her footsteps echoing in the deserted office. "She's wearing a mask, but she's hot."

I take another peek at the phone Becca shoves at me. The Batgirl costume does show off a tall, toned body, and I've always been a sucker for thigh-high boots. "I can't see her face."

"She'll be wearing a costume at the convention. Her face won't matter."

This is why I hired Becca. She's everything I could want in a right-hand woman. "You're ruthless."

She smiles up at me. "And you love me for it."

"I'd give you a raise, but I just gave you one at Christmas."

"I sent Batgirl a message."

I shuffle some papers on my desk, pretending not to care. "Better get home before that husband of yours comes down here."

"Don't worry," Becca says, pausing on her way out. "She'll respond. No one can resist the six-pack."

I wave her out of my office. I'm not worried. Rejection has new meaning after what I've been through. There's a wall of ice around my heart that nothing can penetrate. Not even a sexy Batgirl in skin-tight leather.

Two Conditions

The message from the Holidates app comes through at the worst time imaginable. We are just finishing up an audition for the lead role in this month's independent play. The panel goes silent after a particularly touching rendition of the monologue. You could hear a pin drop.

And then my phone blares with a notification.

All eyes turn to me.

"Sorry!" I whisper-shout and then back off the stage behind the curtain.

I open the app and nearly stumble over a chair. Grabbing onto the nearest thing I can find, I steady myself on the back of a very large, grumpy man, otherwise known as our stage manager, Jason.

"Watch it, Deer Legs," he says.

"Bite Me, Sasquatch." I smile and wave my fingers, pointing straight to my butt.

"You wish," he says in a burly growl.

But I catch the quick smirk under his formidable mustache. Jason loves our banter as much as I do. And Deer

Legs is a compliment compared to some of the nicknames he's assigned to the other crew members. The worst ones are the ones he says behind their backs.

I find a spot away from the rest of the cast and crew and swipe open my Holidates App. So far, the men have been disappointing. Maybe it was my fault. I should have been more specific. I only asked for athletic, tall, and funny.

I should have specified what I didn't want. Cocky, player, asshats need not apply.

This latest guy doesn't even have a head.

His profile picture is a slab of man chest glistening with beads of water.

"Annie!" Jason looks over my shoulder at my phone. "Are you looking at porn?"

I shove my phone in my pocket. "Nosy much?"

"We're not paying you to look at porn backstage." His voice is a deep rumble that matches his size.

"You're not paying me at all," I say. "I'm a volunteer."

He glowers. "They need you out front."

I return my focus to the play, and it isn't until hours later that I remember to check the Holidates app. I'm out with the crew for a drink when my phone dings with a notification.

The headless guy has sent me another message.

> Robinson42: Are you familiar with comic books?

Am I familiar with comic books? Sheesh.

> Portia: Isn't everyone?

> Robinson42: Not me. That's why I need you.

It feels nice to be needed. Even though I've never met this

guy and he might be a total weirdo with a spandex kink or a missing head, I'm intrigued.

The server sets down my mocktail. It's bright pink with a frothy topping shaped like a dome that makes me a little intimidated to actually drink it. I tilt my head to the side to taste it without popping the cute bubble-shaped adornment on top and consider my response to the headless dude.

I'm intrigued, but also slightly wary. I've been known to be a bit impulsive and naive. I never think before falling into a situation, and sometimes I can't get myself out of them.

Portia: What exactly do you need me for?

After I type it, I realize I've set myself up for a pervy response. But I'm not sure how to delete a message on this app, so I steel myself to hear about his wacky demands. Instead, the message I get sends a thrill of excitement racing through me.

Robinson42: I need a date for Total I-Con

My heart flip-flops, and my fingers tremble as I attempt a response. I have to delete and start over several times before I can stop shaking.

Portia: In Vegas?

Robinson42: Yes

Portia: Next week?

Robinson42: That's right

Portia: But it's been sold out for months

Robinson42: I have two tickets.

I don't answer for a while because I am too busy dancing and pumping my fist in the air.

My friends are used to seeing me do all kinds of nutty stuff, including dancing on this very tabletop not long ago. They don't bat an eye at my antics. But a lady at a nearby table eyes me and flags down the server.

"I'll have what she's having," she says.

My high energy level is no thanks to liquor. After a particularly wet December where I consumed way too many adult beverages, I'm doing a dry January. It's going surprisingly well. Not only am I an awesome designated driver, but I've also learned that I don't have to drink to have a good time. A good time finds me even if I'm completely sober.

This seems to be one of those good times. When I pick up my phone again, I see hot torso man has written several messages.

> Robinson42: Are you still there?

> Robinson42: I know it's a lot to ask you to travel and its last minute, but you can have your own room. And I'll pay for everything.

Would it be insanity to go to Vegas with a man I've never met? Probably, yes. Am I going to do it?

Hell yeah!

This is Total I-Con, and I'm a geek. I wouldn't miss it for the world.

> Portia: I'm in. On two conditions

> Robinson42: What?

> Portia: One: Can you help me win a mud run?

Robinson42: I can't make any guarantees, but I'm pretty athletic. I'm tall and I played sports in college.

Portia: Okay

Robinson42: And the second?

Portia: You have to promise me you have a head.

Robinson42: Promise I have a head.

Portia: Great! I'm in!

Gina arrives and sits on the stool next to mine. I throw my arms around her and squeal.

"What the hell is that for?"

I smack both her cheeks with an appreciative kiss, then wipe my lipstick off her face. "I'm going to Vegas, and it's all thanks to you."

Gina glances around the table of our friends and cast mates, but they just shrug. She takes a sip of my drink and nods with approval. "Just making sure you're not sloshed off your first drink of the year."

"I'm one-hundred percent sober, and ten-thousand percent excited."

I fill Gina in on the details, but instead of being excited for me, she's cautious. "Let me see this guy," she says. When I show her the headless wonder, she frowns. "Oh, fuck no. I'm not letting you do this."

I scowl at the screen. He has a perfectly delectable chest, and whatever his head looks like, I'll just have to deal with it. It's not like I'm a super model. My mouth is too big, my hair is too big, and my personality is even bigger.

"I'm sure he's not that ugly," I say.

Gina knocks her knuckles on my forehead. "Hello?

Annie? Is there a sane person in there? I'm not talking about his face. I'm talking about his criminal record. What if he's an axe murderer?"

"They don't let you fly with axes these days," I say.

"What if he's a dick?"

"I'm not marrying him. I'm getting a free trip to Vegas and a ticket to Total I-Con from him."

Gina narrows her eyes at me. "Your parents are never gonna let you do this."

"I'm twenty-seven years old. I can do what I want."

Gina's head tips back as she laughs. "Does your mom know that?"

I've been living on my own for years now, but somehow my parents are still very involved in my life. My mom thinks I should get married, but she also doesn't like any of the men I date. Not that I've had a date for a while, hence the Holidates App.

"What they don't know won't hurt them," I say.

Gina gets ready to argue, then thinks again. "Let me see that picture again."

I pull out my phone and show her the profile picture for Robinson42. I can count each one of his abs individually, and his pecs look hard enough to bounce quarters on.

"He looks pretty fit for forty-two," I say.

Gina shakes her head and hands me back my phone. "Are you sure you want to do this?"

"It was your idea."

"This isn't what I had in mind."

"Relax," I say, sipping my drink and popping a pretzel in my mouth. "What could possibly go wrong?"

CHAPTER 3

Hands Off My Sister

The day just keeps getting worse. Every time the phone rings or I open an email, it's bad news. I'm finding out exactly how many clients Evelyn has stolen. More come out in the open by the hour. Half my clientele is gone. And the other half is going to bail if I don't convince them I can stay afloat with half my clients gone.

I'm so fucked. Everything hinges on Kline and his famous cream for dry butts.

I can't take being in my office for another minute. "Becca?"

"Yeah?"

I roll my eyes and shove a hand through my hair. When did we take to yelling down the hall instead of buzzing each other on the phone? When Evelyn took half our clients and staff. That's when.

With a frustrated huff, I grab my belongings and shove my arms into my coat. "I'm taking off for the day."

Becca looks up from her computer screen with a pinched expression. I can only hope she wasn't looking at our financials.

"It's only three o'clock," she says.

"I realize what time it is."

Her eyes widen and she looks me over with a critical eye. "You look like shit."

My shoulders stiffen under my coat. "Thanks."

"I'm only saying it as a friend."

I force a smile. "Don't worry. I'm not going to drink away my sorrows at happy hour." I check the time. "I'm picking up an old college friend from the airport."

Becca gets up, hurrying after me. "Vince, wait." She puffs as she catches up to me at the elevator. "Geez. Your legs are long."

"Sorry." My brow wrinkles in concern as she catches her breath. "You okay?"

She places a hand on her round belly. "I'm fine." After a quick glance around at the few employees I still pay weekly, she lowers her voice. "I wanted to tell you that it's all taken care of with Portia."

I punch the elevator call button. "Who?"

"Portia from Holidates."

"Who the hell is Portia from Holidates?"

Becca looks at me as if I've lost my mind. "Your date for Total I-Con. You'll be going out early to register, and she will be joining you the night before the convention. I ordered her a dress to wear and booked a dinner at Exalto." She waves her fingers in the air. "It's a premier restaurant. Very exclusive. I booked for four, but it's up to you to get the Klines to come."

"Great." I jab the elevator call button again as if that will make it come any faster. The last thing I want to deal with now is the disaster of my dating life on top of the disaster of my career. "Just email me the details."

Thank God the elevator arrives. I slip inside before Becca can continue the conversation. I don't want to know a thing about Portia, or whoever she is, until I have to.

On the short drive to the airport to pick up Phillip, my old college teammate, I banish work from my mind. It's been too long since I've seen him. Phillip is the reason I settled in North Carolina a few years ago. He'd invited me to his parents' house for Thanksgiving our senior year, and I'd never forgotten how much it had felt like home to me.

The small mountain town of Mossy Oak, North Carolina felt like a dream come true. It was a world away from where I'd grown up in the heart of a big city. The people were welcoming, the town was charming, and Phillip's family was the family I'd always wanted.

Except his sister. I didn't want a sister like her.

Phillip's sister was fucking hot.

Ten years later, I wonder if she still is. And if she's going to be joining us tonight.

Phillip is waiting out front of the small airport for me. Even though it's been a few years since our last college reunion, he hasn't aged a day.

He smothers me with a hug as soon as I get out of the car. He's one of the few people in my life who's taller than me.

"Vinnie," he says, clasping me tightly. "It's been too long."

I slap him on the back a few times, feeling transported back a few decades to when everyone called me Vinnie. Phillip is from a family that hugs a lot. Completely opposite of my family. My dad barely tolerates his children, and my mom left ages ago. Phillip is like the long-lost brother I never had.

"What's up, man? You look like shit."

I muster a laugh, because it's Phillip. "Second time someone's told me that today."

"Truth hurts." Phillip climbs into my car, folding his long legs into the space. "You wanna talk about it?"

I shake my head, and Phillip grins. "You haven't changed a bit."

Unfortunately, that isn't true. Evelyn changed me. She

made me fall in love with her, then she left me and tried to ruin my business. I'll never trust another woman again.

We catch up on gossip, discussing our teammates who got married and had kids, got divorced, moved out of the county. So much has happened since we were in college, but somehow it still feels like yesterday.

Phillip glances out the window and gasps. "What happened to the peach farm?"

I look at the row of newly developed retail space and condominiums where row after row of peach trees used to stand. "The owners sold last year."

"That sucks."

"I know, but the town is growing."

"That sucks even more. I liked Mossy Oak the way it was when I was growing up."

"Don't worry. It still has that small town feel."

"For now."

Phillip sounds as put out as I felt the first time I saw the development spreading. I moved to North Carolina because I loved everything about the community, including the fact that it felt like a different decade, something from the past when neighbors had known each other all their lives and there was a sense of unity. It may have developed, but the people were still small-town awesome.

"You don't have plans for dinner tonight, do you?" Phillip asks as we turn onto the street leading to town.

"No. I was just gonna hang out with you."

"My mom is having everyone over tonight. She's expecting you."

My throat tightens. Phillip's mom had made me feel like part of the family when I'd come home with him for Thanksgiving that year when I couldn't afford a plane ticket home. His entire family had welcomed me with open arms.

Including his gorgeous sister.

"Annie will be there," Phillip says, reading my thoughts. "Don't get any ideas."

I adjust my sunglasses and refuse to look away from the road. "What kind of ideas?"

"Ideas that involve your dick."

I cringe. My dick hasn't been involved with anyone since Evelyn. It hasn't even tingled with excitement since she smashed my heart to bits. But now, thinking of his sister's long, toned legs displayed in a sinfully short mini-skirt, her mass of curly brown hair, and those hot lips that had fastened on mine for a brief but mind-altering kiss before Phillip had interrupted us, my dick is suddenly involved.

"I mean it, Vinnie." Phillip glares at me so hard, I feel my skin crawling. "Hands off my sister."

I don't take my eyes off the street ahead. "Got it."

"Good." Phillip laughs. "I'd hate to have to kick your ass."

"I'd like to see you try." Turning onto the crowded square of Main Street, I slow in front of my favorite bar. Knowing Annie will be at dinner tonight has my nerves unsettled. "Do we have time for a quick drink?"

"Sure." His smile is genuine as he spots the dive bar that boasts twenty-five beers on tap. "Nice to see some things don't change."

I wonder if one of those things is Annie, but I'll find out soon enough.

CHAPTER 4

All Grown Up

Pops is asleep in the recliner, Dad is in the kitchen, and Mom is setting the table with her good dishes. The house smells like roasted meat, cumin, and mint. The sounds of Miles Coltrane drift in from the kitchen where I'm pretty sure my dad is bouncing around to the off kilter beat as he stirs the secret spices into his culinary masterpieces.

Once Phillip gets here, everything will be perfect.

I grab my purse and coat from the armchair and wave goodbye to my mom. "Be back in a bit."

Mom looks up at me with a furrowed brow. "Where are you headed off to? Everyone will be here soon."

I check the time on the clock on the wall. "I'm going to grab Phillip from the airport."

"Nonsense." Mom cocks her head at me, her brow furrowing. "He has a ride."

"But I always get him."

"Not this time."

Picking up Phillip from the airport is my job. Dad cooks, Mom sets the table, Pops naps, and I drive to the airport for Phillip when he's in town. Sometimes we stop for a beer on the ride home. It's our time to catch up before the chaos of our family makes it impossible to carry on a conversation.

"Is Lena getting him?" I ask, trying not to feel irritated.

"No. Not Auntie Lena."

I give my mom a more thorough inspection. She looks the same as always, except something is a little off. A little sparkly. She's wearing her usual high bun on top of her head, but instead of her elastic-waist pants and practical shoes, she's wearing jeans and a red sweater. I assumed it was because Phillip was coming home.

Then I notice the dangly earrings hanging from her earlobes? Mom only wears dangly earrings for special occasions.

And are those the fancy gold placemats?

"Mom? What's going on?"

"Nothing." She adjusts a fork on the setting, then straightens the center piece. "Pops!" She calls into the living room. "Do you have your teeth in?"

He grumbles and settles deeper into the recliner.

"Annie, go check on Pops' teeth, will you?"

I stand my ground and cross my arms over my chest. "Mom?"

She glances up at me absently. "What?"

"Who is getting Phillip from the airport? And why do you care if Pops has his teeth in?" No one in our family cares if Pops presents a full set of teeth or not. We're all used to him gumming his food and mumbling.

"We are having company tonight, Annie." She looks me up and down, wrinkling her nose. "I told you to dress nicely."

I'm wearing leggings and an oversized sweater, my version of dressing up for dinner at my parents' house. "What's wrong with my outfit?"

"You never show off your figure. How do you expect to get married?"

I grind my teeth together, trying to remember my mom was raised in an era where women were expected to marry young and start families.

"The man I marry is going to want more than my body. Plus, I'm not planning on marrying any of my family members."

Mom wags a finger at me, a smile spreading across her face. "It's not just family tonight. Vinnie's coming to dinner."

The front door opens, and Auntie Lena sweeps in with her three teenaged children. There's a whirlwind of activity as everyone talks at once and Pops finally sits upright in the recliner and finds his teeth.

"Who the hell is Vinnie?" I ask.

"Mind your mouth," Mom says, somehow hearing me over all the noise.

I'm almost thirty years old, but my family never seems to get my age right. They either treat me like a kid or an over-the-hill spinster.

Dad comes out of the kitchen wearing his apron and hands me a tray of appetizers to set on the coffee table. I'm laden down with food, trying not to trip over my cousin's dog, who is chasing our ancient tabby cat around the house, when the door opens, and Phillip comes in. He's accompanied by a tall, sandy-haired man who can only be described as one of God's most beautiful creatures. He has a square jaw covered in a day's worth of stubble a few shades darker than his hair, a full mouth, and piercing blue eyes that find mine from across the room despite the chaos.

I nearly drop the tray, and Auntie Lena swoops in to grab it from my hands. "Careful," she says, giving me a knowing look that says she might be twice his age, but that doesn't mean she hasn't taken note of the handsome stranger.

"Annie!" Phillip nearly tackles me in a hug. He picks me

up off my feet and swings me around, so my legs barely miss clipping cousin Sasha in the head.

"Phillip!" I return his tight squeeze and for a moment, the gorgeous Vinnie is forgotten. Phillip hasn't been home in forever. He missed Thanksgiving and Christmas because he was filming on location in Canada. I've been promising to visit him, but I've been so busy at work and the theater, there hasn't been a free moment in my schedule.

Phillip sets me down and moves on to hug the rest of the family. No matter what anyone says, Phillip is obviously the favored child. He's warm, funny, and kind. Not to mention successful and generous. Even though he didn't make Christmas, every single member of the family got an extravagant, personal gift. Phillip is the best brother I could wish for. And even though he's four years older than me, no one would dare say he's past his prime.

He gestures at his friend, who is surveying the lively scene with a bemused expression. "Does everyone remember Vinnie?"

Aunt Lena rushes forward to take Vinnie's coat and offer him a cheeseball. Dad pumps his hand and asks if he's been working out. The teenage cousins don't look up from their phones, the animals speed by, and I simply stare.

I look up into the bluest eyes I've ever seen and feel my world tip. I'm nearly six feet tall, and most men are shorter than me. Not Vinnie. I have to crane my neck to look at him. My heart trips as I gaze into his gorgeous sky-blue eyes.

"Good to see you again, Annie." The deep rumble of his voice sends a ripple of pleasure down my spine.

"Good to see you, too."

My gaze lowers from his amazing eyes to his sensational mouth. The carved lines of his lips are so sensual, so firm. And somewhat familiar. A flicker of a memory comes back to me, and heat fills my cheeks. Did we? No. Surely, I would remember. Surely Phillip would have killed him. Or me. Or both of us. Phillip's tolerance for his friends hitting on me is less than zero.

"How have you been?" he asks.

My gaze flicks from his mouth to his eyes as I try to find the memory of him through the thick fog in my brain. He is so gorgeous, I can't form a single thought, much less an answer to his question.

Luckily, my mom saves the day. "Vinnie! It's been so long. You're a man now."

I stare at Vinnie. Yes, he's a man. Good on you for noticing, Mom. It's not easy to miss those broad shoulders, bulging biceps, and muscled forearms.

"Hi, Mrs. Callis." He chuckles good-naturedly. "Yes, I'm all grown up."

Mom hugs him vigorously, kissing him on both cheeks. "And you remember my Annie," she says. "She's all grown up now, too." Mom winds her arm through mine. "And more beautiful than ever."

Heat blooms on my cheeks. "Mom!"

"What?" She grins up at me. "My baby is stunning!"

I'm hardly a baby, but telling my mom that isn't going to do any good. She will forever think of me as a pre-teen. In need of a husband. Weird, I know, but that's my traditional, old-fashioned family in a nutshell.

"She looks exactly as I remembered," he says, his blue eyes holding mine.

My mom hooks one elbow in Vinnie's arm and the other in mine and steers us into the living room. "Why don't you sit down and get reacquainted?"

She shoves us down onto the loveseat next to each other, then departs into the dining room, although I can still feel her gaze on us.

"Looks like you're stuck with me," I say.

"Can't say I'm unhappy with the situation." His gaze dips down my face, lingering on my lips like a caress.

His voice is a deep rumble, stirring an old memory. I shift closer, trying my best to place him. He smells amazing. His cologne is subtle—refined and expensive, but still rugged. I take another long sniff, hoping his smell will jog a memory.

He narrows his eyes at me. "Are you sniffing me?"

I sniff dramatically a few times, pretending something is itching my nose. "No. That would be weird."

His lips twitch into a smile. "I remember you were kind of weird," he says fondly.

"Yep. That's me," I say with more than a touch of pride. "The quirky little sister."

Sitting so close to Vince makes my skin tingle in the most delightful way. I may not remember him, but I'd like to. He turns toward me, and his hard thigh brushes mine, making more than my skin tingle. He really does smell incredible. I take another long sniff, committing his masculine smell to memory.

"You're definitely sniffing me."

I smile mischievously. "Am I?"

He gives me a long look. "Annie."

I like the way he says my name with a mix of frustration and desire. My smile widens, and I look up at him from under my lashes. "Vinnie."

"I go by Vince these days," he says.

I flutter my eyelashes dramatically. "Vince."

"Do you have something in your eye?"

I allow my rapid blinking to return to normal and laugh at myself. "I'm trying to flirt."

His blue eyes flare, going hot and hungry. "I think we..."

Phillip interrupts us, shoving us apart to sit in between us. The love seat is hardly big enough for me and Vince, and I end up hanging off the side.

"Dad needs you in the kitchen," he says, shoving me to the floor.

I land with a thud, barely missing the edge of the coffee table. Our cat hisses at me from his hiding spot under the table, taking a swipe at my leg.

Vince meets my gaze over Phillip's head and shrugs sheepishly. Something about the gesture rings a bell. A memory tugs at the edges of my mind, and I'm finally able to grab onto it and tug.

Suddenly everything comes flooding back. Ten years ago, Phillip had brought a friend home from college. He'd been funny, charming, and gorgeous. Somehow, we'd ended up making out in the laundry room until we got busted by Phillip.

My heart leaps to my throat as I realize that friend was Vince.

CHAPTER 5

Laundry Room Reunion

In between bites of the most delicious food I've eaten in years, I sneak looks at Phillip's little sister.

I lied about her looking exactly as I remembered. She's even more gorgeous than she was all those years ago. Everything about her is bright and shiny. Her eyes, her hair, her quick wit. Annie just sparkles.

"What made you want to move to Mossy Oak?" Mrs. Callis asks. "If I remember, you were from a big city."

"Chicago." I take a roll and slather it with dill butter. I've already eaten three rolls, but I could easily eat my weight in them. "The rolls are delicious."

"Thank you," Mr. Callis says, puffing up proudly. "I'm better at cooking, but I've been dabbling in baking lately. Wait till you try the baklava."

"Really, George," Mrs. Callis says. "Don't brag. And let the boy answer the question."

I've forgotten what it was. Luckily, Phillip answers for me. "He thought he'd have a better shot here than the city." Phillip laughs. "Didn't know he'd be stuck here for life."

Stuck isn't exactly how I'd describe my situation. "I fell in love with Mossy Oak when I visited here in college." I make eye contact with Annie, who has been watching me as much as I've been watching her throughout dinner. "The people are so nice." My chest squeezes as I think of Evelyn. Not all of them are so nice. But most.

"The people are wonderful," Annie says. "I never want to leave Mossy Oak. Except for traveling, of course."

I finish off my roll, meeting her gaze. "Where do you want to go?"

She sighs, looking dreamy. "Everywhere."

"Everywhere is overrated." Her mother shakes her head. "It's dangerous for a young girl to travel alone."

"I'm not that young," Annie says.

It's been more than ten years since we snuck a kiss in the laundry room. She'd been a high school kid while I was in college, way too young for me. I'd been an asshole for kissing her, but she seemed so much older and more mature than most of the girls I went to college with. When Phillip had caught us, he'd promised to beat my ass and disown me as a friend if I ever made a move on his sister again. Considering he was one of the only guys at school who gave me a chance, I needed him as a friend more than I needed a long-distance girl-friend who was still in high school.

But I never forgot Annie Callis.

And now she's all grown up.

Annie argues good-naturedly with her grandfather, wres-tles her brother for the last roll, and breaks into a spontaneous song and dance while she's helping clear the table.

There's something so sweet about her it brings out my protective side. I can see why Phillip warned me away from her. Annie is too good. Too cute.

She's the exact opposite of Evelyn and her polished sophis-tication.

But damn, those long legs of hers make me wish they were

wrapped around my hips. And those full, pouty lips bring up all kinds of unwanted fantasies.

"Who wants to play Trivial Pursuit?" Mr. Callis asks, heading into the living room.

"I vote Monopoly!" says one of the young cousins.

"Taboo is the best."

As everyone argues over which game to play, Annie catches my eye and gestures discreetly down the hall. Phillip is distracted by the heated debate over which game to play and doesn't notice as we sneak away from the rest of the family.

Against my better judgement, I follow Annie down the hall toward the laundry room, aka, the scene of our kissing crime. She turns around and smiles at me, holding a finger to her lips as she slips inside the room.

The noise of laughter and conversation fades into the background as I follow her into the room. She's standing in between an overflowing basket of clothes and the dryer, leaning casually against the wall.

"You remember this room?" she asks, smiling wickedly.

Heat flashes through me, and desire hums in my bloodstream. "Of course."

Annie takes my hand and tugs me close. "Care for a trip down memory lane?"

She smells delicious, like cinnamon and sugar from the baklava we had for dessert. Her body is slim and strong, with just the right amount of curves that make my dick take notice.

A trip down memory lane is exactly what I need right now. I've been someone else for the past few months. Calloused and reserved, unsure of myself, I've been less than since Evelyn ended our engagement.

With Annie pressed against me, I feel a spark I haven't felt in too long. I wrap my arms around her narrow waist, and she arches against me. Her hard nipples brush my chest, and I realize she's not wearing a bra under her sweater.

My dick is definitely involved now.

Frustration makes my heart pound hard. "I promised Phillip I wouldn't touch you."

She quirks a brow. "Too late."

Her fingers twine through my hair and she tugs my face down to hers. There's a sexy gleam in her dark eyes as she closes the distance between us and kisses me.

Jesus. She is one sexy kisser. Her mouth is soft and full, and she tastes even better than she smells. It's been so long since I've kissed anyone other than Evelyn, I wasn't sure I'd remember how. But one taste of Annie, and my body knows exactly what to do.

Our tongues touch, and a hot slake of lust fires from the point of contact through my entire body. Suddenly I'm burning with the need for more of her. To taste and touch and fill every hollow crevice in my heart with her.

Annie is sweetness and spice. She's everything I've been missing in my life. Everything I need.

A moan escapes her mouth as I slide my tongue against hers, and the sound touches something inside me I thought was gone forever. The kiss turns feverish, and I press her against the dryer, wedging myself between her legs.

She hooks her leg around my calf, angling to get closer. My fingers skim under the hem of her sweater and slide up her smooth skin to cup her breast. She's bare under the sweater, just as I thought, and her nipple stiffens against my palm.

Annie sucks in a breath, arching against me. Her hands slide to my ass, and she squeezes, pulling me closer to her heat. "You feel so good," she says, trailing her lips to my neck.

I grind against her, feeling her melt into me. If we weren't at her parents' house right now, I'd have those skin-tight leggings peeled off her already. I'd be on my knees, burying my face between her thighs.

Guilt lashes like a whip, and I ease back. Because we are at her parents' house, and because—Phillip.

Annie's eyes flutter open, and she blinks up at me. "What's wrong?"

"We have to stop."

"I agree." She wrinkles her nose. "It smells like bleach in here. Not very sexy."

I want to laugh, but I force myself to take another step back. "It's not that."

Her hands slide to my chest. "Don't worry about my family. They won't notice we're gone for another ten minutes or so." She rolls her eyes. "Pops is formidable at trivia. Once he gets going, there's no coming up for air."

I gently remove her hands from the front of my shirt. "Phillip made it very clear he doesn't approve of us."

Annie's eyes flash, and she raises a dark brow. "I don't care what Phillip thinks."

"I do." I tuck my hands into my pockets to keep from touching her. "He's one of my best friends. And I made him a promise."

Annie cocks her head at me, studying my face. "What did you promise?"

I shake my head. "That I wouldn't do this."

Annie's mouth drops open, then she glares at me. Pushing me aside, she pokes her head into the hall. "Phillip?" she calls into the living room. "Phillip! Come here, will you?"

I grab her hand and tug her back into the laundry room. Has the smell of bleach gone to her head? "What the hell are you doing?"

"Don't worry," she says, winking at me. "I'll handle this."

Phillip comes into the laundry room, filling the space with his long, lanky body. He glances from his sister to me, his face closing down in anger. "What is it?"

Annie jabs a finger at her brother. "Did you tell Vince to keep his hands off me?"

"Yeah." Phillip's jaw ticks as he glowers at me. "Looks like he didn't listen."

"Damn straight he didn't listen." Annie grabs my hand and yanks me close to her side. "You can't tell me who to put my hands on," she says. "Watch this."

She grabs my face between her hands and kisses me. I freeze up and don't kiss her back, but after a moment, my body responds despite my best efforts not to. I kiss her back, pressing my lips to hers as if she's the air I need to breathe.

"Annie!" Phillip growls.

But she pays him no mind. Her arms wind around my neck, and she angles her head, deepening the kiss. Pleasure radiates through my entire body. She feels so good pressed against me. So right.

Phillip storms out of the room, and the sound of his footsteps pulls me out of my trance. I untangle myself from Annie's embrace and glance at the doorway where Phillip stood only moments earlier. He's gone. And if I don't do something about it, our friendship will be too. He's my oldest friend, one I can't afford to lose.

"I'm sorry," I say to Annie. "I've got to go."

Annie's laugh sounds behind me. "If you let my brother push you around, you can forget about me."

I hesitate for a split second, then stride into the hall, seeking my friend. Women come and go. They get what they want, then toss the man aside. I'm not losing my friendship with Phillip over his little sister.

No matter how right she feels in my arms.

Texts from Holidates App

Portia: Thank you for the tickets. I'm so excited for this event and everything in Vegas!!

Robinson42: You're welcome. I hope you're a little bit excited to see me too?

Portia: I can't wait to see your face.

Robinson42: And I yours.

Portia: Can you give me a little hint? What color are your eyes?

Robinson42: Blue. Yours? I can't tell from the photo. Maybe you can send me another one?

Portia: I'll show you mine if you show me yours.

Robinson42: Or we could just wait until we meet in Vegas. And let it be a surprise.

Portia: I'm okay with that. But we should discuss costumes. Do you have any ideas?

Robinson42: That's why I need you. Can you come up with something?

Portia: No worries. I've got tons of ideas. Your profile says your stylish. What are you wearing?

Robinson42: Are you trying to sext with me?

Portia: No, I just want to see if you actually are stylish. Because I have a brother and he thinks he's stylish, but he's actually not at all.

Robinson42: I'll send you what I'm wearing today and you be the judge.

Portia: Very impressive. The pocket square is a nice touch. I see you conveniently left off your head again.

Robinson42: Don't want to ruin the mystery. Can you email my assistant your dress and shoe size for a dinner on the first night? And your favorite color.

Portia: I have my own dresses and shoes.

Robinson42: I want to give you something for coming all the way to Vegas with me.

Portia: Thank you. But you've already given me enough.

Robinson42: I haven't even started.

Portia: What else are you going to give me?

Robinson42: That's up to you. In Vegas.

Portia: I'm looking forward to it.

Robinson42: It's cold today, I hope you're wearing something warm. Can you send me a picture?

Portia: Guess what I'm not wearing?

Robinson42: What?

Portia: Socks.

CHAPTER 6

Quasimodo

The airport is like nothing I've ever seen before. There are advertisements everywhere, huge screens showing clips from concerts, shows, and gambling floors.

Geez Louise, I want to do everything. Take it all in. I want the food, the shows, the lights, the music. Most of all, I want to meet Robinson42 and see his face.

While I wait for my luggage at the claim area, I lose track of time watching clips from the amazing shows they are offering. I can't decide between the acrobatic shows and music performers, but what I really want is a Broadway show. If my Holidate wants to go with me, that's great. If not, I'm more than happy to go alone.

I feel like exactly what I am—a small town girl in the big city. A country mouse overwhelmed by the flashing lights and noise.

I'm so absorbed in the big screen advertisements; it takes me a lot longer than it should to realize everyone from my flight has picked up their luggage and the only suitcase left on the carousel is a set of golf clubs. Panic seizes me.

Where is my bag?

Is it missing? Did someone take it?

Holy crap! Our costumes are in my suitcase. They were too big to take in my carry-on bag, so I'd been forced to check them. If my mother would have known I was flying, she would have warned me not to check any bags in case they were lost. But my mother has no idea I'm traveling to Vegas to stay with a man I don't even know for the weekend, who might possibly not have a head. My mother would have put me on lockdown if she'd known. She would have enlisted my father and brother to talk me out of it just in case she couldn't use her mom-guilt on me.

No one knows I'm here except Gina.

I may be stupid for agreeing to meet Robinson42 in Vegas, but there's no turning back now. I'm here, and I'm ready to experience everything Vegas has to offer. With or without the costumes I painstakingly made for Total I-Con.

At least I packed all my other essentials in my carry-on. And thank geez, Rob42 has a dress for me to wear tonight. I'll worry about the costumes tomorrow. I've helped out in the costume department long enough to know the outfit is made by the person wearing it, and also that costumes can come together on any time frame or budget. It's more about attitude than what you're wearing. And I've got plenty of attitude for us both.

"Excuse me," I say to an airport employee pushing a luggage cart. "I think my luggage is lost."

"Don't worry little lady," he says. "It happens all the time, but they always find it."

Hope rises. "Really?"

"Sometimes it takes a year," he says.

Hope sinks like a brick in my belly. "That doesn't help me much."

"I'm kidding," he says, grinning from ear to ear. "It's

usually within six months, tops." He pushes the cart to the side. "Come with me and you can fill out some paperwork. They'll get you fixed up."

"Thanks. You're nice."

"Why wouldn't I be? I live in Vegas, where we make dreams come true."

He leaves me at the office of lost luggage, and I discover everyone else is nice here, too. They promise to find my luggage and deliver it to my hotel by morning. By the time I head outside to get my ride, I'm feeling confident that everything will work out.

The ride to the strip is shorter than I expected. I'd thought all the descriptions of Las Vegas were exaggerations, but the strip is exactly how people describe it. The high-rise hotels pop up out of nowhere, an oasis in the desert. The buildings are lit up even in the middle of the day, and the strip shines like something from another world. The traffic slows us down and gives me plenty of time to crane my neck out the window at all the sights. Rare cars idle at the curbs of hotels, buildings glitter with mirrors and lights, and the sidewalks are crowded with tourists and performers.

I could stay here for weeks and not see everything I want to see.

I make a mental list of everything I want to do. The giant Ferris wheel is number one, and of course, a gondola ride at the Bellagio. And there's no way I'm leaving without a photo in front of the Welcome to Las Vegas sign.

"You can let me out here," I tell the driver, even though we are a few blocks from the hotel. "I want to walk."

"Suit yourself," he says.

I hop out of the car and grab my bag. After a moment, I'm swallowed up by the crowd. It's loud and crazy. Dancers advertising their show are dressed in peacock feather headdresses and little else, and a man with a long white beard rides a unicycle through the crowd. Tourists stop in front of me mid-stride to take photos in front of iconic hotels, and everywhere there is noise. Laughter, music, horns honking, bells ringing. It's all sights and sounds, colors and smells. It's everything I hoped for, and I haven't even set foot on the convention floor where I will be surrounded by like-minded geeks from all over the world.

I walk past my hotel so I can get a selfie in front of the Eiffel Tower, then double back to the lobby.

Inside is just as busy as the sidewalk outside. Travelers, gamblers, drinkers, and shoppers crowd the main floor of the hotel. It smells like a combination of spicy cologne, cigarette smoke, and money. I walk straight up to the clerk without having to wait, as most people are here to shop, ogle, and gamble.

"Checking in?" the clerk asks.

"Annie Callis," I say, handing him my identification and credit card.

He types on his keyboard, then hands me a key. "You're all set. Do you need help with your luggage?"

A dark cloud threatens my good mood, but I push it away. "Unfortunately, my luggage was misplaced."

"Happens all the time," he says, smiling sympathetically. "I'm sure it will be located by the morning."

"Really?"

"Really. We aim to please in Vegas, and that goes for your luggage too." He shows me a map of the enormous hotel. "You're in the Elvis suite," he says, pointing to the map. "It's on one of our nicest. Enjoy your stay."

I meander through the gift shop on my way to the elevator, stalling before it's time to meet Rob42. A cute keychain with an alien face grabs my attention. I buy it for him and make my way to the elevator with a renewed sense of bravery.

It's now or never. No turning back now. Time to meet the mystery man and find out if he's Quasimodo or Clark Kent.

The elevator climbs higher and higher. Each floor we rise adds to the nerves in my belly. My legs feel like wet noodles as I step off the elevator and start down the hall to our suite. I pause at the door to our room, heart hammering in my chest.

I don't know whether I should knock or just go in. Sweat pops out on my forehead and I wipe it away. Now I'm shiny. And I've chewed off my lipstick.

Searching through my purse, I find my lipstick and quickly reapply. It's the best I can do. If my Holidate doesn't like what he sees, too bad. He's stuck with me.

I ball my fist and reach up, tapping loudly on the door.

CHAPTER 7

Under Her Spell

A long day of stalking the registration room pays off, and I *accidentally* run into Mr. and Mrs. Kline picking up their lanyards. I nonchalantly invite them to dinner at a restaurant I happen to have a table for tonight, even though the waiting list is six months long. Happily, they say yes, and now it's time to freshen up before Portia arrives.

Everything hinges on her. The Klines think I'm bringing my new girlfriend, and they are ecstatic that I'm over Evelyn. Word travels fast in the marketing industry, and everyone knows we've split. In fact, they knew Evelyn and I were splitting before I did, seeing how she called them all weeks in advance to pitch her solo venture.

Half of them went with her; half went with me. Kline hadn't decided yet, and that's what this weekend was all about. Convincing him Fastpitch Promotions was the right choice to take his anti-chafing lotion line to the next level. Kline makes it clear that he wants someone who "gets" him. I know he's a family man, obsessed with comic books, but not much else.

Over dinner tonight, I'm hoping Portia will be able to impress him with her geek knowledge and take the pressure off me.

She'll be here in a few hours, and I'd be lying if I said I wasn't nervous. I remind myself again that we only have to pretend to be dating. If we can't stand each other, we never have to see each other again after the mud run. This isn't a real love connection.

Becca has handled all communications with Portia. I barely know anything about her, other than she looks hot in a Batgirl costume. Becca got her plane ticket, selected her outfit for tonight, and chatted her up over text on the app. I don't even have Portia's phone number or know her real name, but I'm trusting my assistant to have selected someone suitable.

Our suite has plenty of room in case we can't stand each other. There are two bedrooms with king-sized beds and luxurious bathrooms, separated by a living area with a wall of windows boasting a view of the strip.

The shower is pure heaven. I stand under the spray of a dozen jets and have to force myself to exit. Portia should be here soon, and I fight off equal waves of excitement and nervousness. Wrapping a luxurious towel around my waist, I lather up for a shave.

For some reason, Evelyn pops into my mind. She always appreciated a close shave. I wonder what she's doing tonight. Is she at home trying to come up with a scheme to steal more of my clients? Or if she's eating takeout by herself, missing me?

Not that I'm missing her in the slightest.

I refuse to think about Evelyn. I won't let her get in my head. I pick up my razor and scrape away the scruff on my chin. Not thinking of her. No way.

"Hello?"

I flinch, and the razor slips, nicking my jaw. I wince at the sudden, intense burst of pain.

"Hello?" the woman's voice calls again, sounding nearer.

My heart pounds as I hear footsteps coming closer. This isn't the first impression I'd hoped to make. Checking the time, I see I've been too long in the shower, and there's no chance this is housekeeping.

I can't decide if I should finish shaving or find some pants. Deciding on the pants, I rush into the bedroom. Then the door creaks open, and it's too late. I'm going to meet Portia with a half-shaved face, dressed only in the world's fluffiest bath towel.

She steps into the room, and the first thing I see are legs for days. I'm still dragging my gaze up the best pair of legs I've ever seen when she speaks, and her familiar voice hits me like a cartoon hammer on top of my head.

"Oh, my Geez! Vinnie?"

My head spins, and my gaze flicks to her face, confirming that those endless legs belong to none other than my best pal's little sister.

"Annie! What the hell are you doing here?"

Her eyes widen as they drop from my face down my body. "Are you Robinson42?" She bursts out laughing. "I thought you were going to be an old man with a spandex fetish."

My heart pounds furiously as I try to make sense of the situation. How can this be happening? Out of all the women on the dating app, I had to get paired up with the one who is off limits.

Annie can't be Portia. But she is.

She looks gorgeous. Her hair is a wild mess of curls, loose around her shoulders, and her wide mouth is stretched in the most infectious smile. Annie is magnetic. Impossible not to like. It's somewhat of a comfort to know the Kline's are going to easily fall under her spell. Just like me.

The smokey sound of her laugh winds around me like a caress. My body responds as if she's running her hands over me. I grasp the towel tighter and will my body to calm down.

"It's my lucky day," she says, striding across the room to hug me. "I'm so happy to see you."

I'm happy to see her, too. I shift my lower half away from her embrace, hoping she can't feel exactly how happy.

She releases me and slowly drops her gaze down my chest. "I thought for sure you photoshopped that six-pack in the profile picture." She reaches out and pokes me cautiously in the stomach, her smile widening. "But you're real."

Her touch wreak havoc with my system. She's so close, I can smell the floral scent of her perfume. Emotions war inside me. I'm glad to see her. So glad it's Annie I will be spending the weekend with and not some stranger.

But I'm also painfully aware of the mess we're in.

I need to set some boundaries so I can resist her incredible charm. Stay strong and keep my hands to myself.

If I don't, Phillip is going to kill me.

CHAPTER 8

The Queen of Bad Decisions

Rob42 has a head. A very handsome head. And very familiar.

"Why didn't you say anything at dinner the other night?" I ask.

Vince's shoulders tense, and his blue eyes turn glacial. "I need to put some clothes on," he says.

He looks fine the way he is, with the towel slung low across his hips, and all those delectable muscles flexing every time he moves. As far as I'm concerned, it's a crime for this man to wear clothes.

"I'll go explore the rest of the suite," I say, giving him some privacy.

I check out the living room, the other bedroom and bathroom, not quite believing my luck. Not only do I get a free weekend in Vegas at the best convention in the world, but I get to spend it with Vince.

He joins me in front of the window overlooking the busy strip, looking casually gorgeous in a pair of gray sweatpants and a T-shirt.

"What are you doing here?" he asks, voice flat and accusatory.

A hum of annoyance spreads through me. "Don't act like this is a surprise."

"Annie, I swear to God, I'm as shocked as you are."

"You sent me the plane ticket." I turn away from the window to face him. "You've seen my real name. You can't possibly be surprised to see me."

"I didn't handle any of my correspondence. My assistant did everything."

My belly clenches. He just might be telling the truth. His face is closed down, but his body gives him away. He leans toward me, eagerness etched in every line of his body. I try not to look down. Because—sweatpants.

I take a step closer to him, inhaling the fresh scent of soap and shampoo.

He takes a step back, putting his hands up. "I think you should go."

I ignore his words and read his body. Really sweatpants, you are not helping the situation. "I think I should stay." I meet his gaze and feel the absolute confusion and terror radiating off him. I can't help but push his buttons. "What are you afraid of?"

His entire body stiffens. "Don't play games," he says. "What would your brother say if he knew we were together?"

I take another step, enjoying the look of desire that crosses his face before he banishes it. "I don't care what Phillip says. He isn't in charge of me."

Vince sidesteps me and puts the sofa between us. "It's too late to change this." He sweeps a hand through his hair, still damp from the shower. "We're stuck."

"Geez, thanks for your enthusiasm." I stare out the window at the darkening sky. Vegas decked out in lights is a sight I've always wanted to see. Vince isn't going to ruin it for me. I want the shows, the music, the performances. I wouldn't mind having a handsome man at my side for it all, but I'm okay with going alone.

"We'll just have to make the most of it."

I watch him walk to the bar cart; my eyes glued to the round globes of his ass. "I plan on it.

He pours himself a glass of amber liquid. "Drink?"

I shake my head. "I'm not drinking all month."

"What? Why?"

"Is that a problem?"

He studies me for a moment, then shakes his head. "That's fine. You'll be my sober wing woman. Keep me from making any bad decisions."

I laugh, because I'm the last person to stop someone from making a bad decision. More likely I'd be the one to suggest it. I'm the queen of questionable decisions. I pull out the keychain I bought him. "I got you a present."

His face brightens, and he looks ten years younger when he smiles. "You did?"

I shrug, trying to downplay the gift. "It's nothing big." Nothing like first class tickets to Vegas and entry to the most exciting event in the world.

He takes the bag I hand him and pulls out the keychain. His brows pucker in confusion, then he lets out a hearty laugh. "Thanks." He glances around, noticing my lack of luggage. "Are they bringing up the rest of your bags?"

My heart sinks. "My checked bag didn't make it." I grab my carry-on. "But I have all the essentials in here."

Vince stares at my small suitcase and pales. "But you have our costumes, right?"

I wince. "They didn't make it." I shoulder my bag and head to the bedroom.

"Wait. What do you mean they didn't make it?"

I walk into the luxurious bedroom, which features a red

velvet draped bed and a hot tub overlooking the skyline. "Don't worry. They assured me the luggage would be found quickly, and they will deliver it to our room."

Vince stops abruptly, his jaw flexing. "Are you saying you don't have our costumes for tomorrow?"

I reach up and pat his cleanly-shaved jaw. "It's going to be alright. This happens all the time in Vegas. They lose luggage." I shrug. "They find it."

Color rises on his cheeks in two bright spots. "What if they don't find it?"

"You're too stressed." I reach out and settle my hands on his shoulders, giving them a quick squeeze. "Good Lord, you are stiffer than a tombstone." I rub vigorously. "Loosen up. It's Vegas."

He glares at me, his shoulders tensing even more under my touch. "What if it doesn't come? Then what? I can't show up without a costume."

"It will show up. But if it doesn't, we'll figure something else out."

He looks so miserable. I reach up on my toes and kiss his cheek. His skin is silky smooth under my lips, and I linger for longer than I intended. Vince draws in a shaky breath and mutters my name in a grunt of frustration. Then his big hands close around my waist and pulls me to his chest, covering my mouth with his.

We stand like that for a long moment, our lips pressed together, neither one of us moving. It's a kiss I've seen in romantic movies dozens of times, but this is real. This is magic.

Then, his mouth moves over mine, and I'm in heaven. He really is the world's best kisser. Other women don't know what they're missing. His lips are warm and soft, and his arms are strong as they wrap around me, lifting me up onto my toes. The first touch of his tongue against my lips makes my head spin and my knees weak. He knows just how to use his mouth to make me want to go on kissing him forever.

I taste whiskey on his tongue, and I feel drunk off the flavor. The spicy scent of his aftershave invades my senses, and the hard press of his body is as unyielding as a mountain. His hands smooth up my back, pressing us together from shoulder to thigh, and I feel *everything*.

"Vince," I moan his name as he pulls back, easing out of the kiss.

He blinks down at me, his gaze slowly clearing from under the haze of desire. His hands slide up to my shoulders, and he grips me firmly. "For fuck's sake, Annie. You're not supposed to be here."

My spine stiffens. "Why not?"

"I was expecting a stranger. Not... you."

It riles me up to think of Vince sharing this weekend with another woman. Buying her clothes, paying for her ticket, treating her to an entire weekend of Total I-Con fun. "I'm very sorry to disappoint you."

Vince grabs my hand, stopping me as I turn around. "Wait." He closes his eyes on a long sigh. "Let's just make the best of this. We have dinner in an hour. I can't stress enough how important it is to make a good impression. Can we just sort this out later?"

"You're stressing enough for both of us." I walk toward my room. "And you might not know this, but your assistant promised me a night out on the town."

Another long-suffering sigh. "Of course she did."

"I'll impress the hell out of your potential clients, but then we are having fun in the city like I was promised."

Vince turns away, heading toward his room. "Whatever you want," he says before slamming the door.

I slam my door in return, shaking all over as I make my

way toward the enormous bed. What a jerk. Just for that I'm making him stay out until dawn.

A black garment bag is laid out on the bed. I unzip it, my head still spinning from Vince's drugging kiss. We are clearly into each other. Nothing my brother says can change the combustible attraction between us.

I catch sight of the dress and for a moment I can't breathe. It's emerald green, with a silk and lace bodice that looks hand sewn. I pull the dress from the bag and feel the heavy weight of it. This isn't just gorgeous. It's vintage. And exactly my style.

Two more bags reveal a pair of shiny gold heels in a size eight and pearl jewelry. The pearls are opaque and shiny, and when I run them through my fingers, I can feel the slight nubs and bumps in their smooth surfaces. They must be genuine.

My belly flutters when I pull out the lacy panties and matching strapless bra. He's gone to a lot of trouble picking out the perfect outfit for Portia. If I wasn't her, I'd be jealous.

CHAPTER 9

The Love of My Life

I knock on the door for the third time, my patience growing thin. We have thirty minutes before we need to meet the Kline's for dinner, and my nerves are getting the best of me.

"Annie?"

The door pulls open with enough force to make the air around me whoosh. Annie stands there, at least I think it's Annie. She looks like a different version of herself.

An elegant, sexy as fuck, royal version of herself.

"What do you think?" she asks, turning around to give me the whole view.

Her hair is twisted into a complicated braid draping over her shoulder, leaving most of her back bare. She's done something with her makeup to make her eyes look big and seductive, and her lips are bold red.

I want to kiss the color right off her mouth, pick her up, and deposit her on the king-sized bed behind her. We wouldn't leave the room all night.

Forcing the erotic image from my mind, I take a step back. "You look stunning."

Her gaze drops over me. "You look good, too."

Desire pulses between us, but I steel myself against it. Tonight is too important to get caught up in Annie's alluring web.

"We should go."

She nods and steps away, returning a moment later with a beaded clutch and a silk wrap. Her brown eyes hold a note of tenderness. "Thank you very much for the beautiful dress." She touches the necklace at her throat. "And the jewelry. It was very thoughtful of you."

I make a mental note to thank Becca for her attention to detail. The outfit is perfect on Annie. "You're welcome."

She steps out of the bedroom and closes the door behind her. "Tell me what you want from me at dinner."

I drag my attention away from Annie and check my pockets for my wallet and room key. "I want you to be my adoring girlfriend."

"Hmm." Annie turns to look at me. "There's a tax on that."

I glance in the mirror over her head, straightening my tie. "A tax?"

She runs her hands up the lapels of my jacket and loops her hands around my neck, dark eyes twinkling with mischief. "A kiss."

My heart stutters. "Annie."

"Just kiss me," she says, her mouth plump and inviting, only inches from mine.

She's so beautiful and sweet. She shines. I want some of that shine to rub off on me. I brush my lips over hers, careful not to mess up her perfect makeup. The kiss lasts one heartbeat, then two, before I pull away and try to regain my composure.

I promised to keep my distance from her, but it is going to be a battle all weekend long.

* * *

We arrive a few minutes before our reservation, but the Klines have beaten us to the table. They are a handsome couple in their fifties who seem completely oblivious to their surroundings. They are so deep in conversation, it takes them a moment to notice Annie and I approaching the table. Once upon a time, I'd dreamed of having a wife I adored who adored me back. But now all I want is to fake my way through dinner and win this account.

"Vince," Mr. Kline says, standing and offering me a hand.

"Hello, Mr. Kline." I nod at his wife. "Mrs. Kline."

"No need to be formal," he says. "Call us Jim and Sadie." He smiles over my shoulder at Annie. "This is the little lady you've told us about?"

"Annie," I say, drawing her forward.

She tucks herself against my side, fitting perfectly as if we were a real couple. We take our seats and engage in small talk for a few minutes as the server approaches to take our drink orders. Annie orders a club soda, I stick to whiskey, and the Klines sip red wine. This restaurant is listed as one of the best places in the city, and we are lucky to have a table. Every single one is full. A pianist plays live music, and the sound of conversation and laughter fill the air.

"I hope you're hungry," I tell the table. "This place is supposed to have the best food in town."

"Not better than Jim's cooking," Sadie says.

Jim's cheeks color with pride. "My bride never stops bragging on me."

Annie drapes her arm over my shoulders. "Vince is amazing in the kitchen," she says, linking hands with me on top of the table for all the see. "But no one can compete with my dad."

"He is pretty amazing," I say, squeezing her hand.

Sadie smiles at us from across the table. "How long have you two been dating?"

Annie looks at me for guidance. My answer is vague. "Off and on for a while. But it's sticking this time."

Jim isn't satisfied. He eyes us with open curiosity. "How did you meet?"

Annie laughs softly, and I'm nervous about what she's going to say. *Not online.* I try to tell her with my eyes. We really should have taken time to go over these ordinary questions. I should be more prepared.

"He's my brother's best friend," Annie says, gazing at me so lovingly I almost fall for it.

"When we were teammates in college, he was kind enough to invite me to his house for Thanksgiving when I had no way to get back home." I turn my attention to Annie, raising my glass to her. "I ended up meeting the love of my life."

Annie's eyes go wide, and I shrug. It might be a stretch calling Annie the love of my life, but I'm all in on this charade.

We order dinner and make more small talk, never touching on anything more personal than our favorite sports teams or seasons.

And then I make my move and ask Kline where he sees his company in two years, and if he sees our agency as part of that team.

"I haven't given much thought to the future other than where I want to spend my vacation time," he says.

"That's perfect. Let me take care of all your marketing needs so you can enjoy yourself."

Jim nods absently, looking over my shoulder. I turn to see what's got his attention and my stomach sinks. I feel sick.

Evelyn is here.

CHAPTER 10

Well, That Was Awkward

Vince is in mid-sentence when suddenly he turns his head and stops talking. I follow his gaze and see an elegant blonde woman wearing a black gown striding toward us. She seems slightly familiar, and then I realize it's her resemblance to Lady Diana. She has silvery-blue eyes that look to have been chipped from ice, perfect posture, and an air of nobility.

Conversation comes to a quick halt before Mr. Kline rises from the table and reaches out, offering his hand to the woman. "Evelyn, so good to see you."

She inclines her head at him, dazzling him with her bright smile. "I was hoping to see you and Mrs. Kline before the convention tomorrow." She sweeps her gaze over Vince, then finally to me.

I feel the slice of her blue eyes as if she's raked her fingernails over my skin. Tension vibrates off Vince in waves. A muscle ticks in his jaw, and he rises much slower than Mr. Kline as if he's drawing up to his full height with deep determination.

"Evelyn." His voice is as sharp as cut glass. "It's a surprise to see you here."

"Really?" She quirks a perfect brow at him. "I can't imagine why. You know I could never miss the biggest comic convention on the continent." Peering past his shoulder, she looks down at me.

I wave my fingers and offer a cheerful hello, trying to breathe some lightness into the situation.

"Will you excuse us?" Vince asks. His glare fixes on Evelyn, and he gestures toward the restaurant exit. "A quick word, Evelyn?"

She nods and loops her arm through Vince's. "I look forward to seeing you tomorrow," she tells the Klines.

They walk briskly away, leaving us to stare after them.

"Well, that was awkward," says Mrs. Kline.

I drag my gaze away from the hostess stand where Vince and Evelyn have disappeared. "What was that all about?"

Mr. Kline narrows his eyes at me. "You don't know?"

I freeze, realizing a good girlfriend would know everything about Vince. Stalling for time, I take a sip of my water. "I didn't realize she'd be here," I say.

Mrs. Kline reaches out to pat my hand. "I'm so sorry, sweetie. It must be hard to see Vince with his ex-fiancée."

Ex-fiancée? I gulp another sip of water and collect my thoughts. It's hard not to feel insanely jealous of Evelyn. She's gorgeous, confident, and seems to have an undeniable effect on Vince. Meanwhile, I'm just the best friend's little sister with enough quirks to make anyone think twice about dating me.

Due to my height and the long legs that go with it, I'm striking, but I'm no classic beauty like Evelyn.

I swallow the lump in my throat as I see Vince coming back from the front of the restaurant. Alone. His face is an unreadable mask, but his body radiates tension. By the time he reaches the table, I feel his energy like a pulsing wave of anger.

He manages a tight smile at the table and takes his seat. "Anyone for dessert?"

"Not me," says Mr. Kline.

"And I have a costume to fit into tomorrow." Mrs. Kline pats her waistline. "I can't wait to see what you're wearing," she says to me.

Vince nearly chokes and covers it with a cough.

"It will be fantastic," I say.

Vince takes care of the check, and we say goodbye to the older couple. When we are alone on the bustling Vegas strip, I study his face. "You know what you need right now?"

He casts a wary gaze at me. "No."

I stop walking and turn to face him. "Perspective."

He arches a brow. "I was thinking along the lines of another glass of whiskey."

Grabbing his hand, I tug him down the sidewalk toward the Ferris wheel. "You might want to wait for that until we are back on the ground."

Vince stiffens, pulling back as I guide him toward the entry to the ride. "I'm not really in the mood."

"I can see that. But you promised me a night of fun in Vegas."

He peers around me, gazing up at the soaring attraction. "This is your idea of fun?"

"For starters."

His gaze returns to mine almost wearily. "And then what?"

I smile mischievously. "You'll have to wait to find out."

A scowl transforms his face. "I've had enough surprises tonight," he says.

My hand settles on his arm, and I feel the tension pouring off him. "You weren't expecting to see Evelyn?"

He winces at the sound of her name. "I should have known she'd find a way to ruin this for me."

I squeeze his bicep in what I hope is a comforting gesture.

"Nothing is ruined yet," I say. "Dinner went well tonight, and you still have tomorrow at the convention to make a good impression."

His shoulders stiffen. "A convention to which we don't have costumes."

I nudge him forward in the line. "I told you not to worry about that. I've got it under control."

Vince sighs. "This isn't a game, Annie."

"I'm not treating it like one. I take Total I-Con very seriously."

He pulls out his wallet and hands over the money for our tickets. "You don't seem overly concerned."

"I'm not." I step into the passenger car and slide over to allow Vince to enter. "The luggage will come."

"You can't possibly know that." He sits down next to me with a huff of exasperation.

The attendant smiles at us and closes the guard rail. Just as we are about to rotate up, a calico cat jumps into the car with us.

"It's your lucky day," the attendant says. "Sammy only chooses the best couples to ride with. And if you don't kiss at the top when he's riding with you, it's bad luck."

Sammy finds a spot he likes on Vince's lap, and to my surprise, Vince allows it. He strokes a hand over Sammy's fur, making him arch his back and purr.

"The cat thinks we're a couple," Vince says as our car lifts into the air.

"Sorry, Sammy." I scoot closer and stroke the cat behind the ears. "We aren't for real."

Vince gives me a warning look. "It's not that you're not attractive," he says.

"I figured that from the way you kissed me."

He swallows hard, his throat working. "You're gorgeous," he says. "And I never forgot you."

"But?" When he doesn't answer, I press him a little harder. Getting to the bottom of Vince isn't easy, but I'm determined. He's the first guy I've been interested in getting to know in ages. "Is it my brother?"

He looks out at the view, his jaw flexing. "Not just that."

I can hear the sadness in his voice, and my heart goes out to him. "Evelyn?"

His gaze flicks to mine then away with a curt nod. "It will be a long time before I let someone else in."

I tear my gaze from Vince and look out at the city of lights beneath us, reminding myself I'm here for the view. Not the man. I've never been in love, and I don't even know if I'm capable of it. Vince checks all my boxes, including being unavailable, which seems to be my preference.

As we slowly rise over the city, I lean over the safety rail to take it all in.

Vince grabs my shoulder, hauling me back in. "Between you and Sammy I'm gonna have a heart attack."

I glance down at the cat snuggled in Vince's lap. "Sammy is too smart to jump."

"And you?" he asks, clamping his arm around my shoulder and pulling me close.

I like it in his arms a little too much. Despite his warnings, I tilt my face up to his. "I'm smart enough to not want bad luck."

Without giving him a chance to back away, I press my mouth to his. He freezes for a moment, then kisses me back.

CHAPTER 11

Die Happily

After the shock of seeing Evelyn at dinner, I wouldn't have thought it was possible to have a good time. But that's because I've never known anyone like Annie.

From kissing her at the top of a Ferris wheel with a cat in my lap, to people watching on the Vegas Strip, to laughing for hours at a hole-in-the-wall comedy club, the entire night has been... fun.

I haven't had fun in so long, I find myself unable to resist her.

"Do you want to come in?" Annie asks when I walk her to her door a few hours past midnight.

It's hard not to get lost in her big brown eyes, which unfortunately are the same color as her brother's. The reminder snaps me back to reality.

"Can't." It's more of a grunt than a word. Damn if I don't want to back her into her room and strip off that sexy dress she's wearing. Becca needs a raise for picking out such a perfect dress for Annie.

67

"I get it." She tosses a teasing look over her shoulder. "Scared Phillip is going to beat you up?"

I laugh for what feels like the millionth time that night. It's a record breaker for sure. Laughter has been more of a dry spell than sex, and that's been months.

Reaching up to loosen my tie, I level Annie with a serious look. "Not at all."

She smirks. "Well, what are you scared of?"

A lump forms in my throat, and I pull my tie off, stuffing it into the pocket of my jacket. I'm scared of losing one of my best friends. And maybe my heart. It's been a rough year, and I don't think the old ticker can take much more. Annie might just do me in. I have a feeling falling for a woman like Annie would be completely different from loving Evelyn.

Annie cups my cheek and brushes her lips over mine, sending a bolt of lust straight through me.

"Phillip is all talk." She slides her lips to my jaw, then down to my neck, pushing at the collar of my shirt. "I don't want to talk anymore, Vince."

My arm slips around her waist, and Phillip be damned, I can't resist his sister.

I haven't felt this turned on in months. One kiss, and I'm ready to peel off Annie's dress and explore every inch of her body.

My promise to Phillip is forgotten as Annie's hands glide down my chest. She pushes my jacket off my shoulders, and I let it fall to the floor behind me. I fill my hands with her, losing control as I back her up into the room.

We are both panting by the time we reach the bed, and I've finally found the damn clasp to her dress. At the back of her neck, there is a little hook, and my fumbling fingers find it even as my heart pounds painfully in my chest, threatening to kill me if I don't get her dress off. And then she's bare to the waist. I suck in a breath as I gaze at her, and it's over. I'm done.

Phillip is going to fucking kill me, but I don't care. I will die happily. Her small, round breasts are tipped with rosy nipples I can't resist. I bend and take one firm peak into my mouth. Annie groans and fists her hands in my hair.

When I swirl my tongue around her nipple and suck, she rewards me with more moans. Those sexy sounds coming out of her mouth fuel the fire burning inside me. I need more of her.

Trailing kisses across her chest, I tease her other nipple, savoring the taste and scent of her. My hands glide up her ribcage to palm her breasts, and she sighs.

Damn, those noises she makes drive me wild. She's so sexy.

I know I shouldn't have started with her, because nothing can make me stop kissing her, touching her, drawing the sounds of pleasure from her mouth.

She reaches for the buttons on my shirt, working them open in jerky movements.

A loud knock on the door of the suite interrupts us.

"Room service?" Annie asks, her eyes hazy with desire.

I shake my head. I didn't order anything. The knock sounds again and a horrible thought ripples through me. What if it's Phillip? I know he's protective as hell, but he wouldn't track us all the way to Vegas, would he?

Annie's face brightens. "It must be my luggage."

I run a hand through my hair, pressing it back into place. "I'll go check."

Sure enough, there's a bellman at the door, apologizing for the late call. I give him a tip and thank him, assuring him he did the right thing.

"I told you it would be okay," Annie says, fastening her dress behind her neck.

"For a minute I thought it might be Phillip."

Annie lets her arms fall. "I can't believe you'd let my brother control you from a thousand miles away."

The mood takes a turn, and tension fills the air. I realize I'm grateful for the interruption. It would have been a mistake to have sex with Annie. Now that we aren't kissing and she's fully dressed, it's much easier to see that. "It's not just Phillip that's stopping me."

"Really?"

"I'm not interested in a fling."

Color blooms in Annie's cheeks. "At least not with me."

"That's not what I meant."

She crosses her arms over her chest. "I know I'm not your usual type."

"I don't have a type."

"But if you did, it wouldn't be me."

"I never said that."

She scoffs and pushes past me into the living area. "You didn't have to."

I grind my teeth together, wishing we never would have started this conversation. There's no way I can win.

"Uh-oh," Annie says.

I follow her into the living room area. "What's wrong?"

"That's not my suitcase," she says.

I grab the luggage tag and read it. Annie's name is printed in large block letters along with her phone number and address. "Are you sure? Luggage can look alike."

She shakes her head, glaring at the black suitcase. "Open it up."

Turning the suitcase on its side, I unzip it and flip it open. It's full of men's clothing. Pants, shirts, shoes, but no costumes.

"Not mine," she says.

I bite back a curse, anger washing through me. It's not Annie's fault the suitcase got lost, but I can't help feeling frustrated. "This was your responsibility."

She chews her lip, looking at the menswear tumbling out of the suitcase as if it's a snake about to bite her. "I know."

I run a hand through my hair, tugging it in frustration. "What now?"

Annie grabs her purse and marches to the door. "Don't worry," she says. "I'll take care of it."

Before I can stop her, she leaves. My heart is lodged in my throat. I'm frustrated and angry, but it's not Annie's fault. Winning the Klines over is my job. Not hers.

I race to the door and hurry to the elevator. But when I reach the lobby, I realize she's gone, and I don't even have her number. There's only one thing I can do. With my heart nearly pounding out of my chest, I pull out my phone and dial Phillip.

CHAPTER 12

Vegas Style

The streets and sidewalks are just as busy at two in the morning as they were before sunset. Maybe busier.

It's easy to get caught up in the bustle of tourists, performers, and locals who undoubtably make the streets their home. I'm not in Mossy Oak anymore. And I'm determined to enjoy every minute of it.

I stop in for a drink at a few different bars. The well experienced bars don't blink an eye when I order mocktails. One place even brings me an elaborate concoction complete with a mini torch at my high-top table. I take in an improv show, listen to a jazz band, and watch a turtle race.

Really, people will bet on anything.

But there's only so long I can avoid my feelings. My annoyance and frustration spike their ugly heads and I'm back to thinking about Vince's rejection. Then, embarrassment joins the party. Being turned down after getting half naked with a guy isn't my idea of a fun time. It's a shame Vince is so intimidated by my brother, because he's the first man I've been attracted to in ages.

If only he wasn't so handsome, so whip smart, and such a good kisser, maybe I'd be less annoyed with his rejection. He said he didn't want a fling, but he didn't ask me what I wanted.

I walk along the strip, taking in the lights, the music, and the shenanigans of my fellow late-night companions, and I realize I don't know what I want.

A fling with a tall, sexy man would be nice. I've never had one of those before. I'd only had the serious types of relationships. The ones that lasted years and drained my essence.

Yep, a fling is definitely more my style. And Vince is the ideal leading man for the role.

Now I just have to warm him up to the idea.

I pass a store where everything is a dollar. It looks very different than the ones I'm used to back home featuring toothpaste and toilet bowl brushes. The glittery items in the window remind me I'm not in North Carolina anymore, but they also spark a brilliant idea. The Vegas-style dollar offerings are perfect for creating cosplay costumes for me and Vince. If I help him win Kline's business, maybe he will see me as more than his best friend's little sister.

An hour later, I've somehow found my way back to my hotel and miraculously remembered the room number even though I paid zero attention earlier. It's nearing dawn, but I'm buzzing with energy as I let myself into the suite and tiptoe across the living area to my room.

"Annie?" Vince's sharp voice rings out in the quiet. "Is that you?"

"Yes."

"Jesus Christ," he says, popping up from the sofa. He

looks haggard. His hair stands up all over his head as if he's been tugging on it, and dark bags cast shadows under his eyes.

I bristle a bit under his inspection. My parents have babied me all my life. I don't need anyone looking out for me. "I can take care of myself."

He scowls at me. "You didn't answer your phone."

I shrug, my shoulders creeping up and staying there. "I didn't even hear it ring."

He marches toward me and gently takes me into his arms. "You had me out of my mind with worry."

His embrace melts my heart. I lean into him, feeling the solid wall of his chest and the strength of his arms around me. I let the packages I'm carrying fall to the floor and wrap my arms around him. He strokes his hand up my back, pressing me closer to his hard body.

"If anything happened to you, I would never forgive myself." He smooths my hair away from my face and tilts my chin up so our eyes meet. "Don't disappear on me again."

I snuggle against him. I could stay like this forever, but there's so much to do. "I need to work on our costumes," I say, smothering a yawn.

"Not tonight," he says, easing back. "Let's get some sleep and we'll tackle it together tomorrow."

My heart melts a little more. "Are you sure? I know it's important."

"I'm just glad you're back and safe." Grabbing my hand, he guides me to my room. "Do me a favor and delete all the messages from me."

I glance down at my notifications and see I missed calls from Phillip. Heat flushes my cheeks. "You called Phillip?"

He grimaces. "How do you think I got your number?"

Not that I care what my brother thinks, but I know Vince does. "He knows about us?"

Vince opens my door and nudges me inside. "There isn't an us," he says.

I step into my room and glance over my shoulder at Vince, noting the regret in his expression before he closes the door. Maybe there isn't an us right now, but I have a strong feeling that's about to change.

CHAPTER 13

Star of the Show

After traveling, staying up all night, and working on our costumes all morning, Annie should be exhausted. Instead, she radiates energy. The woman is practically overflowing with excitement.

When I come back from a session at the hotel gym, she's ready to pounce on me.

"We have to be at the convention in ninety minutes and you're..." She gestures at me, her hands moving frantically in the air. "Sweaty."

I rub a towel over my damp hair. "Working out helps me focus."

"Well, focus on getting yourself cleaned up and into a black suit." She spins on her heel and heads toward her room. "But don't shave. You'll need the scruff."

I can't show up to the convention where everyone is in extreme costumes in a black suit, something I wear on a regular basis.

"Wait," I call, stopping her before she can close the door in my face. "What is the rest of my costume?"

She beams up at me, her eyes sparkling. "You'll see."

Her excitement is contagious. I have to fight the desire to pull her into my arms and kiss her, but it's a bad idea. "What are you wearing?"

She looks down at her clothes, the same ones she was wearing yesterday when she arrived, a mischievous smile on her lips. "Leggings and a sweatshirt."

I link my fingers with hers, giving in to the desire to touch her. "I meant to the convention. What's your costume?"

Her fingers squeeze mine, tugging me closer. "I'll tell you for a price."

The teasing tone of her voice makes my skin tingle. "What price?"

Annie tilts her face up to mine. Even in her bare feet she's so tall, she doesn't have to stretch very much to reach my lips. "A kiss."

Damn. How am I supposed to resist her? I can't look away from her eyes as she steps closer. Phillip had ripped me apart last night when I asked for Annie's number. I'd managed to convince him it was work related, and he'd finally given in. He'd made me swear I wasn't making a move on his sister.

I can't betray him.

Annie shifts closer to me and loops her arms around my neck. "One kiss," she says in a husky voice. "It's not a lot to ask."

One kiss. Maybe it isn't too much.

I bend my neck, lowering my face to hers. Our lips touch, and I feel like I've been struck by lightning. Annie's lips are magic. Her kiss is a slow, steady promise of what could be between us. A spark lights in my chest, catching fire as she deepens the kiss. Her fingers slide into my hair, and she tugs me closer.

Somehow my hands find her ass and squeeze. I pull her against my hips, and we are pressed together from chest to thigh. One kiss is never going to be enough.

She sweeps her tongue into my mouth, and I can feel her heat. Her mouth, her tongue, her body. She's so hot she's going to catch us both on fire.

I take a step into her room, guiding her backwards. I want her in that bed, stripped naked, arching under me.

"That's it." She pulls back, breaks contact. "That's all you get."

I feel like the rug has been pulled out from under my feet, but I smile down at her. "That's all *you* get," I say. "The kiss was your idea."

She opens the door wide and gestures at me to leave. "Take a shower and get dressed. We don't have much time, and you need all of it to wash the stink off you."

I sniff my shirt. I'm not that sweaty. "Aren't you gonna tell me what your costume is?"

"Nope." She closes the door in my face, and I can hear her laughing on the other side.

"You lied." I rap my fist on her door. "You just wanted me to kiss you."

"I know," she says, her laugh weaving a spell around me. "I'm horrible."

But the thing is, she's not. She's a great kisser. The best kisser I've ever had the pleasure of putting my lips against. Nothing has changed in that department over the years. That stolen kiss in the laundry room haunted me for years, and now that Annie is back in my life, it's hard to think about her not being a permanent fixture. I don't want to let her go.

"You better not still be standing at the door," Annie says, her voice barely a whisper coming from the other side.

A smile curves my lips, and I back away.

* * *

Showered and dressed in my black suit, I return to the living area and find Annie wearing a barely-there costume made of… leaves. Something simmers inside me threatening to boil over. Annie looks absolutely amazing.

"Where's the rest of your costume?" I ask, trying not to stare.

"You don't need this," she says, stepping forward and reaching for my tie. She loosens it and pulls it off, then chucks it toward the coffee table. "You smell good." She presses her nose under my jaw and sniffs without even trying to disguise it.

My hands go around her waist, and all that bare skin is mine to touch. Standing so close to her makes me never want to leave this room. I clear my throat, try to remember the reason I'm here. I need to save my business. Beat Evelyn. "We should go," I say. "Don't want to be late."

Annie produces a square of silky fabric and tucks it into my breast pocket. She combs her fingers through my hair and smiles up at me. "You look perfect."

Pleasure invades my senses, and I try not to be too embarrassed by her compliment. I have a hard time accepting praise, but I'm working on it. My inner voice reminds me to say thank you, and the words come out automatically, sounding stiff and unlike me.

Annie laughs. "I didn't mean it like that."

Heat stings my cheeks. "Oh."

"Don't get me wrong," she says, squeezing my bicep. "You're gorgeous. Who wouldn't want a tall, blue-eyed, handsome man? But I meant you're the perfect Lucifer Morningstar." She gestures into the living area. "You're just missing your wings."

I glance at the sofa and my mouth falls open. A pair of giant wings made of ivory feathers spreads over the entire sofa.

They've got to be six feet wide and shimmer under the over-head lights.

"Lucifer?" I ask. "I thought he was the Devil."

"He is." Annie walks over to the sofa and picks up the wings, giving me a good glimpse at her perky ass barely covered by the tiniest skirt made of green vines and discretely placed leaves. "But he was an angel first, and he was Eve's first lover."

Eve. Of course, she's Eve. Her hair is a long tumble of waves, arranged artfully over one shoulder, and her lips are painted seductive red as if she's just bitten into a juicy apple.

I can't believe she's managed to pull this off in such a short amount of time. "You made all this in a few hours?"

She shrugs and motions for me to turn around so she can help me into the harness holding the wings. "I've been behind the scenes in theater so long I know how to save the show."

Behind the scenes isn't where Annie belongs. She deserves to be the star of the show.

CHAPTER 14

Total I-Con

Vince strides through the convention as if he owns the place. He might not know who Lucifer Morningstar is, but he is portraying him naturally. His wings clear a path all around us. The crowd parts, giving us appreciative looks as we walk by. Not trying to brag, but I nailed this. I'm exhausted, but deliriously happy.

Total I-Con is the most exciting place on earth. The costumes range from outrageous, to sexy, to downright scary. No one disappoints. There are people dressed as heroes like Wonder Woman and Lara Croft, but there is also Snow White and Harley Quinn. Anything goes. The more outrageous the better. Snow White and I pose for a photographer with our apples in hand, and Vince cocks a smile in a photo with a gargoyle.

He relies on me to do the talking when anyone approaches, and I'm in my element. I've never felt more confident or more excited. It's like a slice of heaven looking around at all the people geeking out about fabulous fictional characters.

I grab Vince's arm and pull him into a side hug, reaching up to whisper in his ear. "Thank you for this."

He glances down at me, a half-smile on his lips. "No need to thank me. You've done all the work. You made these costumes. You've saved my ass a dozen times." He stops in the middle of the aisle, causing everyone to move around us and his wings. "And you look stunning."

My heart jumps into my throat like a first-time performer taking the stage. "Thank you."

He leans down and kisses me, his lips lingering on mine, tongue briefly parting my lips. I'm not sure if he's just going for it because of our characters, but I don't mind at all. The world is our stage. We are lovers who chose each other despite the barriers. Lucifer and Eve, the forbidden romance.

My lipstick smears on the shadow of his beard, and a lock of sandy hair hangs over his forehead. He looks rakish. So tempting, I nearly think I've been seduced by the Devil himself.

Or maybe I'm just suffering from exhaustion. I'm riding a high right now, but in a few hours, I'm bound to crash.

Oddly enough, I trust the Devil to take care of me when I do. Vince is not only the kind of guy I want to stop and kiss in the middle of a room full of people, but also the kind of guy I'd trust to make sure I got home safely and tucked into bed.

His hand slides down my hip. "How is this skirt staying in place?" he asks. "I keep thinking it's going to slip."

I plant a kiss on his cheek, leaving another mark of my lipstick. "You're hoping it does," I say.

His dark eyebrow quirks. "Maybe I am."

I stare into his blue eyes, for the first time not caring about visiting all the booths, getting autographs from some of my favorite authors, actors, and artists or mingling with like-minded geeks. All I'm thinking about is getting back to the hotel room with Vince, and all the things I want to do with him. To him.

"Hate to interrupt," a deep voice calls out. "But I gotta say, I love the costumes. You two are great."

I turn to see a furry figure looming over us. It's impossible to see the man under the costume and headpiece, but his voice is familiar.

"Mr. Kline," Vince says, offering his hand to the man's paw. "Thank you so much. Annie is completely responsible for this." He sweeps a hand over our costumes, beaming. "She's a genius."

The furry head bobs. "I think we have a lot in common, Vince. A happy partner is the best partner. And I can see you and Annie make each other happy. Just like me and Sadie."

I look over his furry shoulder and see a woman in a purple bodysuit with horns protruding from her blonde, well-coifed head pursuing a vendor's table nearby. She lifts her hand and waves and I realize under the face paint and wig is Mrs. Kline. She looks amazing. I wave back, and we exchange nods of appreciation.

"I've made my decision," Mr. Kline says. "The account is yours."

A slow smile spreads over Vince's face, and he grabs Mr. Kline's paw again, pumping it with enthusiasm. "You won't regret this."

Mr. Kline's head bobs again. "See that I don't."

When Mr. Kline's wife calls him over, Vince grabs me and pulls me out of the crowd to a small alcove. He tugs me outside onto a balcony and pulls me into his arms. His wings surround us, keeping us in a cocoon of privacy.

"You did it," he says. "You saved me."

I shake my head. "It was all you, Vince."

He takes my chin and tilts my head up. "Thank you."

"You're welcome."

And then his lips are on mine. Crashing and burning in a fiery explosion. His arms wrap around me, and he yanks me against his body. I don't know how he managed to find a dark corner in the bustling conference, but he has, and he uses it to his advantage. He presses my back against the building and kisses me until I'm weak in the knees.

There's nothing I want more than to keep doing this all night. And more.

He backs away before I'm ready, and I lean forward, chasing his lips.

"Let's get you back inside before I get carried away." He takes my hand and brings it to his lips, kissing my fingers. "I promised you a fun time tonight and we aren't leaving until you get every autograph you want and take a million more pictures."

"Really?"

"Of course. Who is the number one person you want to see?"

I can think of a dozen. It's too hard to pick just one. Vince reads my indecision and nods. "Even though I want to stay out here kissing you for a lot longer, we are going back inside, and you will take all the time you need and meet everyone you want."

I wind my arms around his waist, mindful of the wings, and gaze up at him. "What if I say I want to stay here, kissing you for the rest of the night?"

His eyes glimmer, and his lips quirk in a grin. "Any other time I wouldn't mind that. But I know how much you want to be here. I want you to enjoy every moment of this weekend, including what comes later tonight."

My entire body tingles at the suggestion. I press closer to him, feeling the heat of his body beneath his crisp white shirt. "Is that a promise?"

"If you'll have me."

The gruffness of his voice surprises me. "We have the whole night," I say.

Disappointment flashes in his eyes before he glances away. "I'll take it." He kisses me again with fiery passion.

When he breaks away, I wobble on my heels and take in a deep breath, trying to grab my equilibrium. This man is addictive, but I'm at Total I-Con and I may never have this experience again. Plus, he promised me we'd have all night.

We make our way off the balcony to the convention hall and nearly run into an elegant woman dressed as Elsa as we exit.

It takes me off guard to realize it's Evelyn. Her blue velvet dress with the fur trim hugs her body in a way Disney never imagined, and her hair is twisted into an elaborate braid wrapped around her head, leaving her long, graceful neck exposed.

"Hello Vince," she says, ignoring me. "You're missing the convention out there on the balcony."

Vince stiffens and reaches his arm around my waist, cinching me to his side. "You're blocking the door."

She smiles and steps out of the way, sweeping her long dress away from her feet. "Did you have a chance to think about what we discussed last night?"

Vince pauses and gazes at something behind Evelyn, then transfers his penetrating glare back to her face. "Answer is no," he says.

Evelyn steps closer to him. "You're going to regret this."

He shrugs. "Only thing I regret is you."

We step around Evelyn and join the flow of people. "Vince," Evelyn calls after us.

Vince doesn't stop. He guides me along through the foot traffic, parting the crowd with his shimmering white wings. "Forget about her," he says, fingers tightening around my waist. "This is our day."

CHAPTER 15
Cone-ly Ever After

nnie leads me around the convention hall, getting autographs, posing for pictures, and buying souvenirs. The crowd is beginning to thin as the night wears on. By the time Annie is ready to leave, some of the vendors are packing up, and my wings have grown cumbersome. I've knocked over more people than I care to admit. But I'm not the only one in an oversized costume. There is a T-Rex with a long tail, a mermaid being pulled in a wagon turned aquarium, and a giant marshmallow bumping into everyone.

When Annie smothers a yawn, I suggest it might be time to go. She reluctantly agrees. "My feet are killing me in these shoes."

She's wearing the sky-high heels Becca bought her that make her nearly as tall as me. Annie is all legs, every inch of them gorgeous.

As we head to the exit, I see a vendor selling fresh-churned ice cream. It reminds me of home. Ice cream in the summer is one of the few good memories I have of growing up.

"One last stop?" I ask, tugging Annie toward the vendor.

She gazes up at the sign over the arched entrance to the booth and chuckles. "Cone-ly Ever After? Vince, this is a wedding chapel."

I glance at the over-the-top decor advertising chilled bliss. There's a sign that says free ice cream cones come with every marriage. "It's just a joke," I say.

Annie's face lights up. "This is so cute. Look at the cake toppers!" She points at a banana split down the middle made to look like a couple tying the knot.

I shake my head in disbelief. "I'll never understand this town."

"It's easy," she says. "Everything is fake."

"So, what do you say?" I ask. "Will you have a fake wedding with me and an ice cream cone?"

"Marriage isn't a joke," she says, narrowing her eyes at me.

Annie is usually effervescent with excited energy, but I sense the seriousness in her tone. "I agree."

"I'll only get married once," she says. "Like my parents. I want the real deal."

"Well, good thing this is just a scoop of ice cream." I point to the menu selection. "What's your flavor?"

She studies the menu. "I'll take raspberry cream."

I order double chocolate fudge, and Annie takes a moment to fill out the survey while an attendant scoops up our flavors of choice. We pose for a quick photo under the flowered arch and trade licks of decadent homemade ice cream while our photograph prints.

"I like yours better," she says, tracing her tongue along the top of my cone.

I watch her lick the chocolate off her lip and feel the stir of desire. I've given up on trying to resist her. "I think it's time I take my wife to bed."

Annie takes another long, slow lick of my ice cream and grins. "Way past time."

We leave without grabbing our commemorative photo. We don't speak to anyone as we make our way through the lobby to the elevators. It dawns on me that I'm completely sober, but I feel drunk on life. Being with Annie is exhilarating. Her energy is contagious.

She gives me a long look in the elevator, a sexy grin on her lips. "Your appendages are very impressive."

My wings practically take up the entire elevator. A few people squeeze in, pushing me and Annie even closer together. Just before the door closes, Mr. and Mrs. Kline get in. He's taken off his furry head and holds it under his arm like a helmet. What little hair he has on his head is matted down with dried sweat.

"Was that you two I just saw at Cone-ly Ever After?" His gaze flicks from me to Annie.

"It was," Annie replies. "I highly recommend the double chocolate fudge." Her gaze locks on mine, and I don't have to guess what she's thinking. Desire is written all over her face, and not for chocolate ice cream.

"We're so happy for you!" Mrs. Kline leans in and gives Annie a kiss on the cheek. "He better make you happy."

Annie and I smile and nod, pretending along with them that we just had a legitimate waffle cone wedding. "Thank you."

The elevator stops and the doors open. Before they get out, Mr. Kline turns around and gives me a thumbs up. "I'll be in touch on Monday. And I expect an invitation to the celebration back home."

"Thank you." My drunken giddiness just upped another few points. I've saved the business, and it's mostly due to the amazing woman next to me. Kline wouldn't have given me his account if not for the success of this weekend. And that's all thanks to Annie.

When the elevator opens on our floor, I finagle myself and my wings into the hall and fish my room key out of my pocket. My heart pounds hard in my chest as we near our room. I'm about to betray my best friend and possibly ruin our relationship forever. My steps slow as the devil inside me wages war on the loyal friend. Phillip has always been there for me. He helped me make friends in college when otherwise I would have sat in my dorm room all alone. All the guys on the baseball team were friends, but Phillip and I had been like family.

He was one of the few people I kept in touch with from college, one of the few I trusted. And I'm going to throw that relationship away for one night with his sister.

Annie walks in front of me, glancing over her shoulder at me with bright eyes. "This is the best day ever," she says, a grin splitting her face. She spreads her arms wide, gesturing at the elaborately papered walls. "I freaking love Vegas."

My heart squeezes painfully because for a moment I thought she was going to say she loved me. She doesn't even know me, so that's not realistic. Then why do I feel like I'm already half in love with her? Maybe it's those long legs of hers? Or her enthusiasm for everything under the sun?

She stops in front of our room. I have the key ready, but my hands shake as I try to fit it into the slot. This is it. No turning back. As soon as I open that door, my relationship with my best friend from college is over.

Annie places her hand over mine. "Aren't you forgetting something?"

I turn to her, trying not to bump her with my wings. "What?"

"I'm your wife." She puts her hand on my chest. "Shouldn't you carry me over the threshold?"

My blood hums at the sound of her calling herself my

wife. I'd thought that title was going to Evelyn, but I'm so glad I never gave it to her. It sounds so much better on Annie. A tingle runs down my spine, and I push the door open, stopping it with my foot. Even though we both know it's just pretend, I sweep Annie into my arms and carry her into the room.

She winds her arms around my neck and holds on, laughing as I stride into the room. "I don't think a man has ever picked me up before."

"I'm not just any man," I say, carrying her through the living room straight to my bedroom. "I'm your husband."

Her dark eyes meet mine as I set her down on the floor. "I'm only getting married once," she says, continuing with the joke. "So, you're stuck with me."

"Happy to be stuck with you." I cup her cheeks and bend to kiss her. When our lips touch, I feel the connection down to my bones. I'm dizzy with the sensation of her soft lips rubbing mine. Annie is pure electricity, sizzling my nerves every time we touch.

I coax her lips open, and she makes a soft sound of pleasure and presses against me. I deepen the kiss, craving more of her sighs, more of her flesh against mine.

Her lips part for mine, and the quick tease of her tongue darts into my mouth. I taste the lingering chocolate on her tongue. She's sweet and hot, and I want to devour her. I take my time, kissing her thoroughly, tasting and exploring every corner of her mouth.

My wings knock against the dresser as I walk her backwards to the bed. Annie reaches behind me, freeing me from the harness fastening them to my back. I let them drop to the floor, then reach for her again.

Annie laughs as I fumble with her costume and pushes me down to the bed. "Let me do that."

She reaches behind her back and unties the strings holding

together the scraps of her costume. One shimmy later, and she's wearing only a pair of lacy panties and high heels. I suck in a breath, letting my gaze drift over her body.

Annie gives me a little push, and I fall back onto the bed. She steps in between my legs and slides her hands under the lapels of my jacket, easing it off my shoulders. "My husband is wearing entirely too many clothes."

"So is my wife." I run my hands over her hips, slipping my thumbs under the sides of her lace panties. Her skin is silky soft, and I'm careful to be gentle with her. She's a bright, shiny treasure. Something to be cherished.

I drink in the sight of her pale skin, shimmering in the lamplight. Her rosy nipples pebble under my gaze, and a flush spreads up her chest. She's delicately built with fine bones and satin skin. Even though I know Annie is nearing thirty years old, there's an innocence about her.

An innocence I am going to rob. I feel like a dirty dog. Not only for breaking my promise to Phillip, but for taking advantage of Annie tonight. I don't want just one night with her. I want more. And taking her to bed is going to ruin everything.

A sudden wave of guilt crashes over me, and I can't force my thoughts away from all the damage we'd do if we keep going.

I reach up and take her hands, prying them away from my shirt. "I can't."

She blinks at me, her big, dark eyes filling with confusion. "You can't?"

I shake my head, leaning away from her and looking everywhere but at her. One more look at her gorgeous body, and I won't be able to resist. "I'm sorry."

Stepping back, she gapes at me. Her face stricken with horror.

I would stand and try to console her, but the rigid erection in my pants would give me away. "I just can't, Annie."

She covers her chest with her hands and backs toward the door, nearly tripping over my wings. I want to reach for her, to help her regain her balance, but I know better than to touch her. Instead, I let her go, wincing as she slams the door to her room behind her.

CHAPTER 16

Mrs. Castillo

Sleep comes easier than it should considering the huge humiliation I've suffered. But sleep doesn't stick around, and I'm awakened a few hours later, my mind turning over everything that's happened in the last twenty-four hours. From the shock of seeing Vince as Robinson42, to the fun of the convention, and the rejection, it's been quite an eventful day.

I've got whiplash from Vince's sudden rejection. Everything had been going so well.

The convention had been a success. Vince had gotten what he'd been after. He'd beat Evelyn and won Kline's business. Guess that was all he wanted. He certainly hadn't wanted me.

The persistent ringing of the phone on my nightstand drags me from my thoughts. I reach for the phone, but by the time I grab it, the caller has given up.

All I want to do is close my eyes and go back to sleep, but it's no use. I'm awake and reliving every humiliating moment from last night. My bruised emotions hurt like a broken bone.

I squeeze my eyes shut as if that could block out the images of Vince's rejection.

But it isn't in my nature to let anything get me down. After a few minutes of wallowing in self-pity, I remember I haven't really lost anything.

So what if Vince rejected me? It isn't the first time, and it won't be the last. I've been told I'm too tall, too quirky, too mouthy.

Clearly, Vince is a boob man. I don't have a lot going on up top, so maybe that's why he rejected me. I may not have a big chest, but I've got legs for days, and I plan to show off every inch of them in my short pajama set. Let him see what he's missing out on.

After brushing my teeth and rinsing my face, I strut into the living area, making sure to give as much cheek as possible.

But Vince is gone.

His door is open, and his bedroom is cleared out. The jerk had the nerve to leave without saying goodbye. I stalk through his room, hoping maybe he left me a note or something. But every trace of him is gone. The only thing he left is the lingering masculine scent of his cologne and the wings I'd made him.

I'd thought for a quick minute that Vince was one of the good guys. I'd never been more wrong.

A knock on the door to the suite startles me. I'm shamefully hopeful it's Vince and he's locked out. But it's just the bellman, standing in the hall next to a familiar black suitcase.

My luggage has arrived.

He wheels it in for me, then offers a large envelope. "This was left for you at the front desk."

"Thanks." I take the envelope and grab my purse to offer him a tip. "Looks like my luggage came just in time to go home."

He frowns. "Sorry about that. I hope it didn't ruin your stay."

"No worries." I grab some bills from my wallet and offer

him a handful.

"No thank you," he says, holding up his hands. "Your husband gave me a big tip earlier."

"He's not my husband." A shiver of indignation trips down my spine. At least the marriage had been only pretend. I can't imagine being stuck with a jerk like Vince. Even if he is a sexy jerk.

"Well, he's a great tipper," the bellman says. "I appreciate the generosity and hope you come back to see us soon."

After he leaves, I make myself a cup of coffee and carry it to the window where I look out over the city. They say New York never sleeps, but Vegas doesn't get much beauty rest either. I sip my coffee and watch the people down below enjoying everything the City of Sin has to offer.

There's no way I'm letting Vince ruin my trip to Vegas. My flight doesn't leave until the afternoon, I have a late checkout, and I haven't even placed a single bet. I need to hit the town.

After getting dressed, I head downstairs and proceed to win over a thousand dollars at the tables. Take that Vince! I could have been your lucky charm.

When my time is up, I head back to the room and grab my luggage. I spot the envelope the bellman gave me, and rip it open, wondering who left me something at the front desk.

Inside the envelope is a folded piece of pastel pink paper. Despite the unorthodox color, the document looks quite official. It's a marriage certificate listing me and Vince Castillo as husband and wife. There's a picture of us standing under the cotton candy arch with our arms around each other, smiling into each other's eyes.

I think it's got to be a joke, but then I see the official seal of a Nevada notary and my mouth goes dry. It looks like the fake wedding in the ice cream shop wasn't so fake after all. I'm Mrs. Castillo. Vince and I are actually married.

CHAPTER 17

Fully Capable of Performing

I keep my face neutral as Mr. Kline mentions Annie for the third time during our meeting. He wants to take us to dinner now that we are back in Mossy Oak, but I'm not sure Annie will even talk to me, much less accompany me to dinner. I've got to think of a way to fix things between us. Not only for Mr. Kline, but for me.

I miss her like crazy, and I'm ready to admit I want more than just sex with her. I want to risk Phillip's wrath and make Annie mine.

"Let me know when we can grab that dinner with your pretty wife," Kline says as I walk him to the elevator.

"Of course. Love to." I don't bother telling him Annie and I aren't really married. I'll think of something later. First, I have to apologize and win her back. I'll have to make things up to her by winning her company's mud run this weekend.

"Annie is perfect for you." Kline frowns. "So much more than Evelyn."

My chest tightens, and my body braces all over. I miss Annie so badly. Knowing we can't be together is killing me. "Yes. You're right."

101

Leaving without saying goodbye was such a dick move. I really wrecked things. I've tried phoning, but she won't take my calls. She's all I can think about. Her smile, her big brown eyes, her mile long legs—Annie consumes my mind.

"Seeing the two of you together was the reason I decided to trust you with our account. Not just anyone will do for No More Monkey Butt Crack Cream."

I force a smile, inwardly cringing at the name of his bestselling product. Changing the name is going to be my first suggestion. "Thank you. I look forward to a long, happy relationship."

"And I wish you and your new bride all the happiness."

When Kline is gone, I stand at the elevator for a long moment, lost in thought. Then the elevator doors open again, and I have to blink a few times to make sure the woman striding into the lobby is who I think she is.

Annie is dressed in a tight yellow tube dress that barely comes to the top of her thighs. A salmon pink rectangular hat sits on top of her head, and thigh high boots make her legs look incredible. God, I'm a sucker for tall boots on a gorgeous woman.

Her gaze sweeps around the office, halting immediately when it lands on me. Tension radiates between us, and that gut punch I feel every time I think about her feels a whole lot worse in person.

"Annie." A smile spreads across my lips as I take in her crazy outfit. The words "No. 2" are printed down the front of her dress, and I'm guessing that wacky hat is an eraser. "Are you supposed to be a pencil?"

Two bright spots of color bloom on her cheeks, and her eyes narrow. She shoots daggers at me, striding toward me until she's practically in my face. She jabs a finger at my chest. "Why haven't you been returning my calls?"

Confusion draws my brows together. "You didn't call me."

She pulls her phone from the front of her tight dress and shows me the screen. "I've been calling you for two days. You've been ignoring me."

I pull my phone from my pocket and scroll through the recent calls. Her number doesn't show up. I reach for her hand, but she jerks it away. "*I've* been calling you for two days and you haven't answered."

She's so angry there is practically steam rising from her head. "I want a divorce."

The entire staff of six people turns to gape at us. My skin feels like it's on fire with all the eyeballs staring me down.

I refrain from reminding her we aren't actually married. Has she lost her eraser-topped mind? "Maybe we should talk about this in private."

"I'm only getting married once, and it's not going to be to someone who's..." She stops mid-sentence. Waving in the direction of my crotch, she lowers her voice to a whisper-shout. "Impotent."

A collective gasp from our onlookers fills the office, and then silence blankets us. I glance away from my curious employees and pull Annie into my office. Every muscle in my body is shaking as I close and lock the door. "First of all, we aren't really married. Second of all, I'm fully capable of performing."

Annie scoffs, lifting her chin to glare at me. She's over six feet in those boots, and her pink hat gives her even more height. "First of all, we *are* legally married by the state of Nevada. If you would answer your phone, you would know that. And you deleted the Holidates app."

I jerk a hand through my hair, tugging on the short strands. "I told you, I haven't gotten any texts or calls from you. And I deleted the app because I didn't need it anymore. I got you."

Annie's brows draw together, then her eyes go wide. "Phillip! That funky cheeseball! He gave me the wrong number for you on purpose."

Phillip has been sabotaging us from the start. Maybe I should rethink my loyalty to him.

Annie marches across the room, her hips swaying in the short dress. She isn't a traditional beauty, she's too bold for that, too unique. Her mouth is a little too wide, and her jawline is sharp. She may not be conventional, but Annie is unforgettable. Absolutely mesmerizing.

She waves her hands in the air, gesturing passionately as usual. "I want an annulment."

"Because you think I can't get it up?" I can't help but laugh. I have the opposite problem around her. Keeping it down.

"Because I'm only getting married once in my life. You being impotent is just a bonus so we can get an annulment. I looked up the rules, and we don't fit any of the other categories. Unfortunately, I was completely sober and not coerced into marrying you."

I stalk across the room, and take her hand, pulling her to my chest. "My dick works fine," I say in a low growl.

Her eyes widen, and a little sound escapes her mouth. That sound pushes me straight over the edge. I don't give her a chance to answer before I bend my neck and crush my mouth to hers.

She responds like she always does to my kisses, with full Annie enthusiasm. There's no denying the explosion of chemistry between us. Her hands wind around my neck, my tongue slips into her mouth, and we stumble backwards until we land in a tangle of limbs on the expensive leather sofa reserved for clients. I've never even sat on the sofa before, but I am thankful I sprang for something comfortable as Annie lands hard on top of me.

I love the feel of her soft, willowy body on top of mine. She's all legs, wrapping them around me as we fumble for dominance, kissing the hell out of each other.

Our mouths crash together, our tongues tangling with greedy licks. Annie loops her leg around my hips, and I flip our positions, wedging myself between her thighs. Her hand glides over my ass, and she pulls me closer.

I kiss her ear, her throat, her shoulder, anywhere I can get.

Her fingers tangle in my hair, and she jerks my head back, pinning me with her sharp brown eyes. "I thought you didn't want me."

Sweat beads on my brow as I think of what an ass I've been. "Of course I want you."

She reaches for my fly, stroking her hand over my straining dick. "I can feel that. But you rejected me."

I groan as she rubs me through my pants. I want her so badly, it hurts. "Only because you are so perfect for me."

She laughs, and the sound weaves a spell around my heart. "You make absolutely no sense."

Hiking up her skirt, I skim my hands over her bare thighs. "And you're dressed as a pencil."

"Vince." Her eyes are full of pain. "I don't understand you."

I close my eyes and feel the swell of emotions in my chest. "I've tried so hard to resist you, but..."

She cups my face in her hands and kisses me tenderly. Her mouth is warm and soft, coaxing life back into my soul. "Stop trying."

"But..."

"If you mention my brother right now, so help me..."

I steal her words with a kiss. My heart pounds as if I'm fighting for my life. Annie is everything I need. Everything I've ever wanted. I kiss her as if she's the very air I need to breathe. She takes everything I have to give and matches me, demanding more.

I trail a path of kisses up her neck to her ear. "Are we really married?"

"Yes." She breathes hard. "Sort of. We haven't consummated it yet. But the marriage is legal."

Lowering my head to hers, I kiss her again, taking my time to explore every inch of her gorgeous mouth. She's so sexy when we kiss. The little noises of pleasure she makes drive me wild. "This is nuts."

She nibbles on my lower lip, her teeth scraping against my tender flesh. "I know."

"We can't be married." But part of me wants it more than I've ever wanted anything. Annie in my life forever would mean we are family. She would be mine.

"We're not *really* married," she says, her eyes twinkling. "You know. Because of your little problem."

I grip her ass and pull her tightly against my crotch. "I don't have a problem."

Her grin widens. "Prove it."

CHAPTER 18

Try This Thing Out

My challenge echoes off the high ceilings of Vince's office. Then, silence.

His blue eyes find mine. Desire pulses between us, growing stronger with each heartbeat. Vince braces one arm beside my head on the couch cushion and trails his other hand up my thigh.

Fireworks explode along my skin wherever he touches me. I lift my hips, begging for him to touch higher, closer to where I ache for him.

His eyes dip over my face, lingering on my lips like a caress. "We shouldn't do this here."

My chest pinches, and I get a bad burning feeling in my gut. "Are you rejecting me again?"

He eases back, taking away his touch. "This is my office. I'm at work."

I glance around the neat, clean space. It's modern with plush, expensive furniture. Vince must look sexy as hell sitting behind his desk in his well-fitting suit, telling everyone what to do.

I tug him back down on top of me where his solid weight feels so dang good. "Do you want me to go?"

He groans as I wrap my arms around him. "No."

"You own this business," I say, pulling his mouth back to mine. "You can have sex with your wife in your office. You earned the right."

His hand is back on my thigh, then higher, teasing me with slow, gentle movements. "My wife." His gravelly voice brings goosebumps to my skin. "I like the sound of that, Annie."

My pencil costume rucks up around my waist, my panties disappear, and somehow my hands find Vince's zipper. His hot flesh is in my fist, and I can't believe how good he feels.

He kisses me passionately, his tongue thrusting into my mouth, his teeth nipping at my lips. I stroke him mercilessly, pumping his hard flesh until he stiffens like velvet steel. He plays just as dirty, working me with his fingers and his mouth until all rational thoughts leave my head. I coax him toward my entrance, no longer caring about the consequences.

All I know is I want him.

Common sense vacates the premises as he pushes his perfect cock inside me, no barriers between us. He fills me up, makes me whole, completes me like no one has ever done before. His body is a solid weight on top of mine, his mouth is a searing hot brand, his cock claiming with every deep thrust.

Pleasure builds inside me, a speeding train with no brakes. He hooks my leg over his hips and drives deeper, filling me with relentless strokes. He kisses me, and kisses me, and kisses me. Drugging me with his sexy lips. His hot mouth never leaves mine as he makes love to me, murmuring sexy words of encouragement in between slow kisses.

I'm losing control. Every sensation magnifies as he plays me perfectly, burying himself deep, then pulling out with slow, long drags of his heavy cock.

"Come for me," he says, tracing his tongue along my neck. "Wife."

I spiral out with this one word. It sounds so sexy in Vince's low, rough voice. His teeth scrape at my throat as I cry out. As he plunges into me, hard and fast, waves of pleasure crash over me until I shudder uncontrollably. On the last tremble of my orgasm, Vince pulls out. His eyes close, and his throat works as he pumps into his hand. Spots of color rise on his cheeks, and his mouth falls open as he spills his release. Pleasure makes him shiver and break out in a light sweat.

It's the most erotic thing I've ever seen.

When it's over and we are both still, Vince strips out of his shirt and uses it to clean himself up. His actions are in slow motion, as if he's moving through quicksand. When he finally raises his eyes to mine, I see the sadness and regret written all over his face.

His naked chest has me mesmerized, and I'm still a little woozy from what was quite possibly the quickest orgasm I've ever had. Quick, but very effective. This must be what it feels like to win a race. Not that I would know. I've never won an athletic competition before in my life.

"This is a giant mess," he says, glancing quickly away from where I'm sprawled on his leather couch, my pencil costume stuck around my waist.

I drag my gaze away from his chest and throw my legs to the floor, straightening my clothes as I stand. My dress is no worse for the wear, but I feel completely blind-sided. I hadn't been wrong about me and Vince. We are amazing together. Combustible chemistry. But he's right about one thing: this is a giant mess. I can't even get an annulment now.

"I never thought I would get a divorce," I say, my voice wavering as tears fill my eyes.

Vince tosses his soiled shirt aside and pulls open a drawer at the bottom of his desk where he has a stash of new shirts still in their packages. He rips open the plastic and takes out a fresh shirt. "We could try this thing out."

"This thing?" I stifle a frustrated laugh and grab my eraser hat from the floor beside the desk where I didn't even realize it had fallen off. My face is flaming hot with outrage, and my heart slams in my chest. "This thing is a marriage!"

Vince steps forward and slips his arm around my waist. When he pulls me forward and kisses me, my anger dulls, replaced by rekindled desire. His tongue slides along my lower lip, an enticing tease.

If he keeps kissing me like this, I'm going to forget why I wanted a divorce in the first place.

"Give me three months," he says, easing back from the kiss. "Then I'll give you a divorce, no arguments."

My head spins. "Three months? Why three months?"

He kisses me softly, his lips a warm caress that make me want more. "I think we make a good team."

Pleasure hums through me. Maybe we do make a pretty good team. But I don't want to think about the future right now. "I've got to get back to the theater for the next show."

"What is it?" He gestures at my outfit, a confused expression on his face.

"A dark comedy about a back-to-school special gone wrong."

He smothers a laugh. "It never ends with you, does it?"

I raise my brows. "You married me."

"I must have been out of my mind."

"Or didn't realize you were doing it."

He grins. "Sounds about right."

I pat my dress into place. "Look, we don't have to continue this. We can end it now. Just say we made a mistake, get a divorce, and voila, we are free of each other."

"I like being stuck with you." His eyes implore me. "Just give us a chance."

My mouth hangs open. He can't be serious. "I don't know."

His face brightens. "When we win the mud run, you'll see how good of a team we can be."

"If we win, I might consider it."

Confidence shines in his blue eyes. "We'll win."

I stride toward the door. "I'll see you there Saturday."

"Wait." He grabs my hand and spins me around. "Kiss me goodbye."

He lowers his face to mine and claims my mouth in a kiss that makes my head spin. His tongue sweeps into my mouth, teasing and tasting in that way he has of making me lose my mind.

Maybe being married to this man isn't such a bad thing after all.

CHAPTER 19

Second Place

I arrive early to the mud run to get my head in the game. It's been a long time since I competed at a sport, but I remember how important it is to set your mind before an event. I sit in my car with the stereo playing, focusing my thoughts on winning.

I've studied the course on the website, and although they don't disclose all the obstacles, I know the main part of the race is a maze with four entrances. Three of the paths have extra challenges along the way, but one leads straight to the final obstacle. Finally, the race ends in a one-hundred-meter dash. In order to win, both teammates need to cross the finish line.

Even if I have to carry Annie over the finish line, we are winning.

A knock on my window startles me. I turn and see a bald man peering into my window, a wide grin on his face.

"Nice car," he says when I open the door and climb out of my vintage Mustang GT.

I push the alien keychain deep into one of the pockets on my cargo pants. "Thanks."

He strokes his pointy goatee. "Original paint color?"

I nod. The Tahoe turquoise exterior matches the interior, and the chrome accents are polished to a high sheen. "She's the love of my life," I say.

Annie approaches, clad in a fisherman's wading suit complete with rubber boots. There are two black stripes painted across her cheekbones as if she's getting ready for the big game. She's so adorable, I can't hide my grin. "That is until I met my wife."

"Your wife?" The man turns and sees Annie, then looks back at me, his mouth falling open. "She told me she was seeing someone, but she never mentioned she got married."

"We're newlyweds."

He swallows so hard his Adam's Apple bobs in his throat. I almost feel sorry for him. Almost.

Annie joins us, and I put my arm around her shoulders. "You look great. Love the outfit."

"Really?" Her brow wrinkles, brown eyes crinkling in the corners. "I wasn't sure what to wear. I've never done one of these before."

I lean down and kiss her lips lightly. "Nervous?"

She gazes up at me with wide brown eyes. "Terrified."

"Don't be." I kiss her again because I can't resist how cute she looks or how good this feels. "It's gonna be fun."

The bald man clears his throat. "You're married?"

"Hi, Harry," Annie says, as if she's just noticing him for the first time. "This is Vince. I told you about him."

He makes a choking noise. "I can't believe you married this guy," Harry says. "You just started dating him a few weeks ago."

Annie's cheeks turn pink, and she lifts her chin. "Actually, we've known each other for years."

"You've never even talked about him," Harry says.

"Maybe you weren't listening." Annie takes my hand and tugs me toward the field where contestants are starting to gather. "Come on. If we hurry we can get a pre-race smoothie."

I wave at Harry, who is staring at us in disbelief. "See you at the finish line, pal."

"He's so annoying," Annie says as soon as we are out of earshot.

"Ex-boyfriend of yours?"

"He wishes." She barks out a laugh. "Actually, he's the reason I joined the Holidates app. I needed a date to make him back off."

I slip my arm around her waist. "And you got a husband."

"A lot more than I bargained for." Her words are stern, but her eyes are soft. "I still think this is crazy."

"Let's get you a smoothie," I say, changing the subject. "Gotta fuel up to win."

After we down our smoothies, it's time to line up for the race to start. There are hundreds of people here, and I drag Annie to the front of the line. We need to get in a good position to win.

When the gun goes off, I take off at a sprint. Annie nearly falls, and I grab her around the waist so she doesn't get trampled by the crowd.

"You okay?" I run with her cinched to my side, practically carrying her.

"I'm fine. You can put me down."

I set her down and we take off at a run, only slowing when we see the first obstacle a hundred feet away. It's a slip and slide under a tangle of wiry cords. We have to duck and crawl through the mud on our bellies. Annie stays right behind me, benefiting from the path I make in the mud with my bigger body.

"I lost a boot," she says as we run toward the next obstacle.

"It happens. Don't worry."

My confidence bolsters us both. We make a mad dash for the second obstacle, a nearly vertical wall we have to scale with rope ladders. I boost Annie up so that she's already halfway up the wall before she has to start climbing, then follow after her. At the top of the wall is a sheer drop over the other side. Annie is fearless, launching herself over the top and grabbing a rope to slide down.

We are in the top dozen participants as we approach the mud maze. I choose the second entrance, and we run into the maze only to find ourselves at a dead end minutes later.

"Follow the wall to your left," Annie says.

"Are you sure?"

She shrugs, giving me a confused look. "I heard it somewhere."

We double back and start again. Following the left wall works, and before we know it, we are at the exit. It was easier than I expected, but we still have the final obstacle to go, then the sprint to the finish.

"You first," I say, urging Annie onto the log.

She takes a moment to shed her other rubber boot, then approaches the log on bare feet. She's got to be freezing, but at this point it doesn't matter, we are one minute away from winning. No other teams are in sight.

Annie sprints across the log, then turns to cheer me on. She jumps up and down in the mud as I make my way across the treacherous log. Maybe it's easier in bare feet. I slip all over the place, falling in the mud three times before making it across.

When I'm almost at the end, Annie can't contain herself. "One more sprint and we win!"

Just before I exit the log, I slip and roll my ankle. The pain is so sharp, I feel it through my entire body. I push the pain away and get to my feet, determined to make it to the finish line first.

But the searing pain in my ankle stops me short.

It's an old injury, the same ankle I broke in college that ended my baseball career. I'd thought I might make it to the big time, but my badly broken ankle had required surgery that made me miss the second half of my senior season. By the time I recovered, it was over for me. I never played baseball again.

The familiar shame and disappointment wash over me as I see other teams exiting the maze and approaching the log run. If I crawl on my hands and knees, I might make it, but it isn't looking good.

Annie tries to support my weight, but it's no use. I'm too heavy.

"My stupid ankle." I should have been more careful.

"Are you badly hurt?" Annie asks.

"I'm fine, but I can't walk."

"I'll carry you."

Annie tries to pick me up, but I swat her away. "I'll hobble."

A man sprints by us, followed by a woman. We are going to lose. Harry runs by us, looking triumphant, and my heart sinks.

This is it. The end of the race, and we aren't going to win. Suddenly Annie stops trying to drag me.

"It's okay," she says.

Frustration is a tight knot in my chest. "No it's not. We lost."

Annie wraps her arms around my waist and hugs me. "We still have each other."

Confusion fogs my brain. I can't lose the race. I can't lose *her*. "But you said you'd stay married to me if we win."

"I didn't say I would divorce you if we didn't."

She reaches up to kiss me and the celebration from the winners drops away.

It's only us. And for the first time in my life, coming in second feels a lot like winning.

Epilogue

TWO MONTHS LATER

The Mossy Oak airport was first built in the early 1970s when Sky Valley Vineyards became the chosen resort of the rich and famous. The wonderful climate, gorgeous scenery and Carolina blue skies attracted thousands of people a year to the world-renowned winery, and the resort made it even more accessible by funding an airport.

The nearby airport made Phillip's visits more convenient. Since he'd been made head sound technician on a television show filmed in Vancouver, Canada, we didn't get to see him as often as we'd like, but when he did visit, it was only a fifteen-minute drive to pick him up at the airport.

Getting Phillip from the airport was usually my job. But I didn't mind sharing it with Vince. It was time my brother knew about our relationship, and what better way to break it to him than in person?

As we pull up to the airport, Vince wipes his hands on his jeans and shoots me a worried look.

I reach over and pull him close, giving him a quick kiss.

"Don't sweat it," I say. "Phillip doesn't have any say in our relationship."

He grimaces. "That doesn't help."

I twine my fingers through the hair at the nape of his neck. It's soft and luxurious, and I love touching it, knowing he's all mine. "I'm a grown woman. I make my own decisions. And I choose you."

He smiles against my lips. "Happy to be stuck with you."

The kiss turns heated, but I pull away, knowing there will be time with my husband later. All the time in the world.

Spotting Phillip on the sidewalk, I hop out of the car and run to greet him with a hug.

"Annie!"

He does his customary pick up and swing. The fellow travelers on the sidewalk have to watch out for my feet as they go flying in the air.

"Put me down," I say, sputtering with laughter. "I'm going to hurt someone."

"I can't tell you how glad I am you begged me to come home again." Phillip puts me down and grabs his carry-on suitcase. "The weather in North Carolina this time of year blows Canada away." He lifts his face to the cloudless blue sky and inhales a deep breath. "I missed this mountain air."

"We missed you, too."

"Pops better be ready with the Trivial Pursuit. I've been studying." He gives me his best concerned big brother expression. "What was so urgent you needed me home? Everything okay?"

I stiffen as I glance at my car over Phillip's shoulder and see Vince climbing out. "Everything is fine."

Phillip lets out a relieved sigh. "Pops isn't sick? He's getting so old."

"He's been old for decades, but he still beats us all at Trivial Pursuit."

Phillip turns and sees Vince for the first time. I watch his face go from excited, to confused, to suspicious in the span of three seconds. Phillip has always worn his emotions on his sleeve. His gaze flicks to me, then back to Vince. "What the hell are you doing here?"

Vince's jaw clenches, and his face pales. He's been dreading this reunion for a week, ever since I told him Phillip was coming.

And although I sympathize with him over risking his friendship, I am also sick and tired of being treated like a child.

"We're together." My words slice through the tension, clearing up any doubt that Phillip may have had about why Vince is here. I grab Vince's hand and link our fingers together. "We thought you should know."

Phillip's mouth twists, and he glares at me. "You could have told me on the phone instead of insisting I come here on my one weekend off."

I glare back at my brother, unbothered by the frosty glint in his familiar brown eyes. "What happened to being happy to breathe the mountain air?"

Bright spots of color bloom on Phillip's pale cheeks. "The air reeks of betrayal."

I laugh. "Always bringing the drama, bro."

Phillip doubles down on his glare. "I just call it like I see it, Fannie. I don't like this."

My skin crawls at the sound of my hated childhood nickname, but I let it slide. "I don't care if you like this." I turn to Vince and smile encouragingly. He's so cute, even when he's trying to disappear into the sidewalk. "Vince doesn't care either."

Vince clears his throat. "That's not true. I'm really sorry, man. Sorry that you don't approve." He straightens his shoulders, drawing himself up to his full height. "But I'm not sorry about falling in love with Annie."

"Aww!" I reach up and pat his cheek. "You're the cutest."

He grins at me. "Thanks."

"For God's sake," Phillip says. "Stop making googly eyes at each other. It makes me want to gag."

I pop the trunk for Phillip's luggage. "Don't puke in my car. I still haven't forgiven you from that time you barfed chicken nuggets all over my new ride."

Phillip unceremoniously throws his suitcase into the trunk. "That car was a piece of shit before the chicken nuggets. And it was your fault for making me ride The Corkscrew. I told you it was going to make me sick."

Without another word, Phillip climbs into the backseat and closes the door. Vince stares at the door, his brow wrinkling. "That wasn't so bad."

"Told you so." I give his bicep a squeeze as I scoot around the front of the car. "And my parents already love you, so telling them will be a breeze."

Tonight, we are announcing we are officially a couple. Our Vegas marriage is still top secret.

For the last two months, I've been having the time of my life dating my husband. Vince is always up for a good time, he supports me in every imaginable way, and our chemistry is off the charts. He's the man I want to come home to. The man I want to see first thing in the morning.

I might be a little obsessed with my accidental husband.

While I drive to my parents' house, neither one of the men in my life does much talking. I gladly carry the conversation, giving Phillip some time to digest the news and Vince a chance to prepare for the rest of the Callis crew.

It's bound to be a wild night. Mom has invited everyone in the family, Dad is cooking up a storm, and Pops has a new set of dentures he wants to show off. Auntie Lena will be there with her children, the pets will be running savage, and everyone will be talking at once.

There are multiple cars in the driveway when I pull up to my parents' house, and I wonder who else is invited for Phillip's visit. Our family motto has always been "the more, the merrier," and I'm sure my parents are in a state of bliss with a full house.

"Do mom and dad know about the two of you?" Phillip asks as I park next to Aunt Lena's dented minivan.

"We are telling them tonight," Vince says.

Phillip grunts. "Great."

"Mom is going to be ecstatic," I say. "It will take some of the pressure off you and your non-existent dating life."

Inside the house, the usual chaos greets us. Mom and dad are surprised to see Vince, but the major attraction is Phillip. Everyone makes a beeline for my brother, smothering him with attention.

Vince puts his arm around me and pulls me aside. "Care to join me in the laundry room?"

A thrill runs through me. Sneaking a moment in the laundry room with Vince? The answer will always be yes. I grab his hand and drag him down the hall. We've come so far since the last time we stole away to the paradise of freshly washed clothes.

In the privacy of the laundry room, my husband pulls me into his arms and kisses me breathless. Our kissing chemistry never ceases to amaze me. I could kiss this man for the rest of my days on earth. Happily forsaking all others. His mouth was made for mine.

He pushes me against the dryer and curls his hand around my neck, deepening the kiss. His tongue parts my lips, and his taste is in my mouth. Sweet and spicy, I can't get enough of him. My heart pounds, and a smile builds in my chest. I feel giddy from his touch. I never want this kiss to stop.

"Annie," Vince says my name against my lips. "This isn't going to work."

The serious tone in his voice makes my chest pinch. "What?"

He releases me and takes a step back. I miss his warmth immediately, and my pulse pounds so loudly in my ears, I can't think straight. Is he ending this?

My heart breaks, and I gulp in air. I didn't want to actually marry Vince, but now I can't imagine my life without him. I look forward to spending time with him, to eventually moving in together and producing taller-than-average, geeky, but athletic children.

Is it all over?

Just as I'm steeling myself for his rejection, he drops down to one knee and pulls a velvet box from his shirt pocket.

My hands fly to my face. "Oh, my Geez!"

Vince stares up at me, his blue eyes earnest in his serious face. "Annie Callis, I love you more every single day. I know you are technically already my wife, but I want to make it official. Will you..."

Vince doesn't get to finish the question before I sink down to the floor and throw my arms around his neck. "Yes."

We fall onto the floor in a tangle of limbs and lips, laughing as we knock over a laundry basket full of dirty clothes. He manages to push the ring onto my finger in between kisses. It's a dazzling diamond in a unique, antique setting.

It's perfect. He's perfect. We're perfect.

"When did you get this ring?" I stare down at it, noting it looks vintage. Definitely from a different era.

He lifts my hand and looks at the sparkling ring on my fourth finger. "It was my grandmother's. She gave it to me years ago. Told me to find someone special to wear it." His gaze lifts to mine. "I'm so glad I found you."

I frame his face in my hands and kiss him. He shifts our

positions, rolling me on top of him so the cold tile floor is against his back, not mine. My husband is such a gentleman.

"I can't wait to be your wife."

He laughs and pulls me back down for another kiss. "You already are."

"What's this?"

I look up and see Pops standing in the doorway of the laundry room, his new teeth hanging out of his mouth. Behind him, my entire family peers down at us. I grin and lift my left hand in the air, waving the diamond.

My mom squeals, my dad shouts, and Auntie Lena swears. The dog barks, the cat chases him off, and my cousin tears his gaze away from his phone long enough to roll his eyes at our ridiculousness.

Phillip reaches down and offers his hand to Vince. "Welcome to the family," he says. "Looks like you're stuck with this crazy bunch."

Vince takes my brother's hand and smiles at me. "There's no place I'd rather be."

WANT MORE SMALL TOWN STEAMY READS BY JILL BRASHEAR?

Sign up for Jill's Newsletter and get a free copy of Riley's Love Connection.

Riley has had a crush on Josh since the day she met him in pre-school when she saved him from a bully trying to steal his teddy bear. At the time, he was a skinny kid who was too shy to stand up for himself. Now, he's a six-foot tall firefighter whose muscles have muscles.

Riley thinks Josh doesn't know she's alive. She couldn't be more wrong.

Read *Riley's Love Connection* for free now!

Acknowledgments

This book was so fun to write! Anytime I thought of something crazy that would never happen in real life, I threw it into this book. I was able to cut loose and have a blast with this over-the-top romantic comedy!

I'm so thankful to my sprinting buddies! We somehow found each other even though we are from different corners of the world. Vicki, Tara, Linda, Angela, Carrie, Angel—you made this book so much better and the writing far less lonely.

Thanks to my family for all their support. Grace and Michael, you're the best! Everything I do is for you. Grace—I hope I'm a great "ro model." Michael—Thanks for the stock tips. In case this book doesn't take off, at least I have ETC to fall back on. Tarzan and Mickey, I love you! Thanks for the daily entertainment and dose of joy!

About the Author

Jill Brashear is a hopeless romantic and author of swoon-worthy contemporary romances that will leave you breathless. With a pen in her hand and a heart full of love, Jill weaves tales of passion, longing, and happily-ever-afters that will make your heart skip a beat.

Also by Jill Brashear

ALOHA SERIES

Try Easy

Try Me

Try Right

Try Over

BLUE RIDGE BOOK CLUB SERIES

Love, Lacey Donovan

XOXO, Valentina

Blue Collar Crush

Sincerely, Thatcher Hayes

Regards, Mia

STANDALONES

Win, Lose, or Love

www.ingramcontent.com/pod-product-compliance
Lightning Source LLC
Chambersburg PA
CBHW070404200726

48294CB00003B/1081